Dahl, Michael.
The Green Queen of Mean
/
c2010.
33305242997991
mi   08/01/19

D0460432

PRINCESS CANDY

THE GREEN QUEEN OF MEAN

STONE ARCH BOOKS
a capstone imprint

Princess Candy

THE GREEN QUEEN OF MEAN

WRITTEN BY
MICHAEL DAHL & SCOTT NICKEL

ILLUSTRATED BY
JEFF CROWTHER

DESIGNER: **BRANN GARVEY**   ART DIRECTOR: **BOB LENTZ**

SERIES EDITOR: **DONALD LEMKE**   CREATIVE DIRECTOR: **HEATHER KINDSETH**

ASSOC. EDITOR: **SEAN TULIEN**   EDITORIAL DIRECTOR: **MICHAEL DAHL**

PRODUCTION SPECIALIST: **MICHELLE BIEDSCHEID**

Graphic Sparks are published by Stone Arch Books a Capstone Imprint 151 Good Counsel Drive, P.O. Box 669 Mankato, Minnesota 56002 www.capstonepub.com Copyright © 2010 by Stone Arch Books All rights reserved. No part of this publication may be reproduced in whole or in part, or stored in a retrieval system, or transmitted in any form or by any means, electronic, mechanical, photocopying, recording, or otherwise, without written permission of the publisher.

Library of Congress Cataloging-in-Publication Data
Dahl, Michael.
  The Green Queen of Mean / by Michael Dahl [and] by Scott Nickel ; illustrated by Jeff Crowther.
    p. cm. – (Graphic sparks. Princess Candy)
  ISBN 978-1-4342-1893-3 (library binding)   ISBN 978-1-4342-2803-1 (paperback)
  1. Graphic novels. [1. Graphic novels. 2. Superheroes–Fiction. 3. Environmental protection–Fiction. 4. Schools–Fiction.] I. Nickel, Scott. II. Crowther, Jeff, ill. III. Title.
  PZ7.7.D34Gr 2010
  741.5'973–dc22   2009029808

Summary: The teacher, Mr. Slink, assigns an environmental project, and Halo Nightly pairs up with Flora, the school's resident tree hugger. Their team has the assignment in the bag (reusable, of course). But when the evil Doozie Hiss ruins their chances for a good grade, Flora changes from happy hippie to eco-terror. With her superpowered candies, Halo faces off against the Green Queen of Mean!

Printed in the United States of America in Stevens Point, Wisconsin.

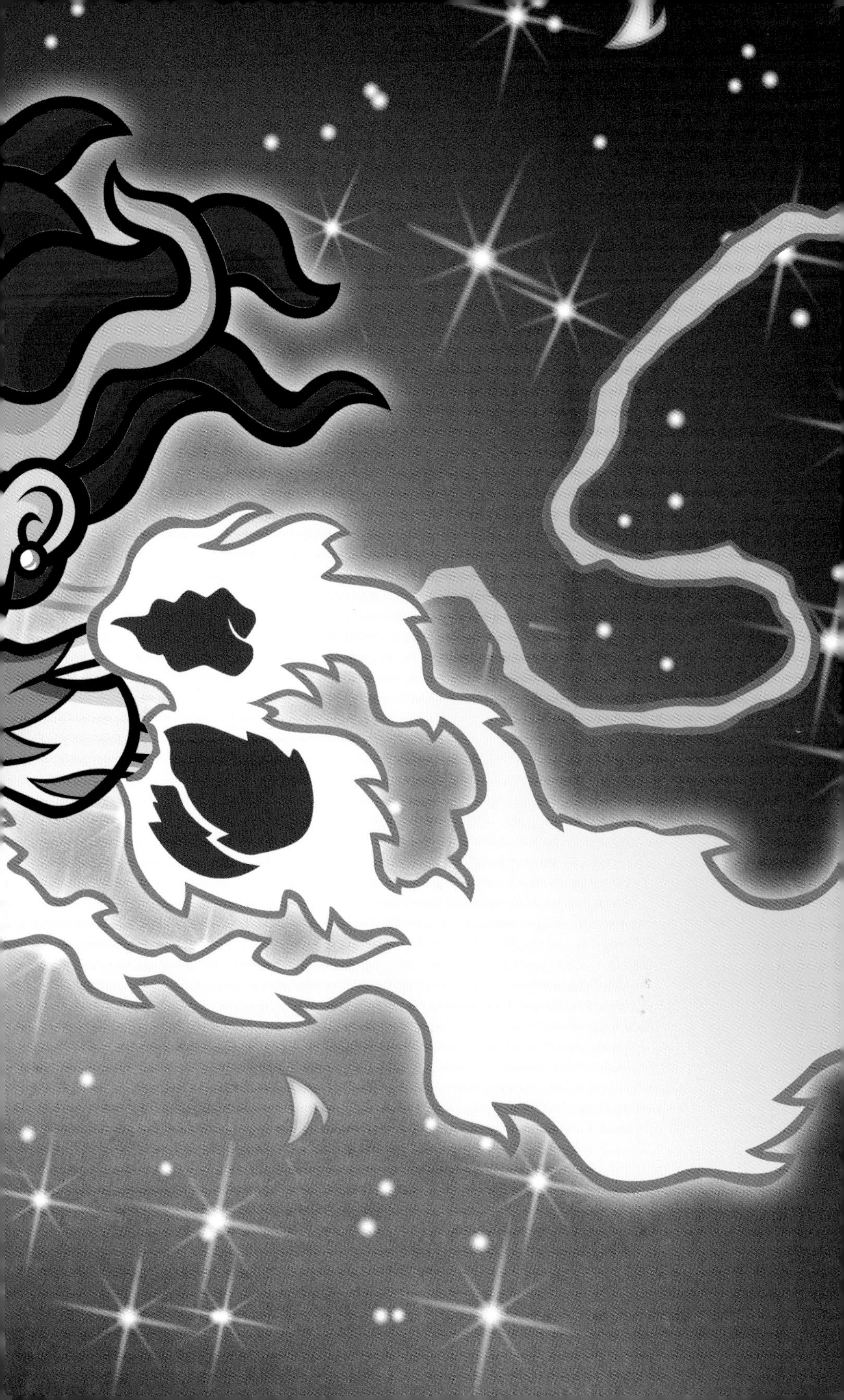

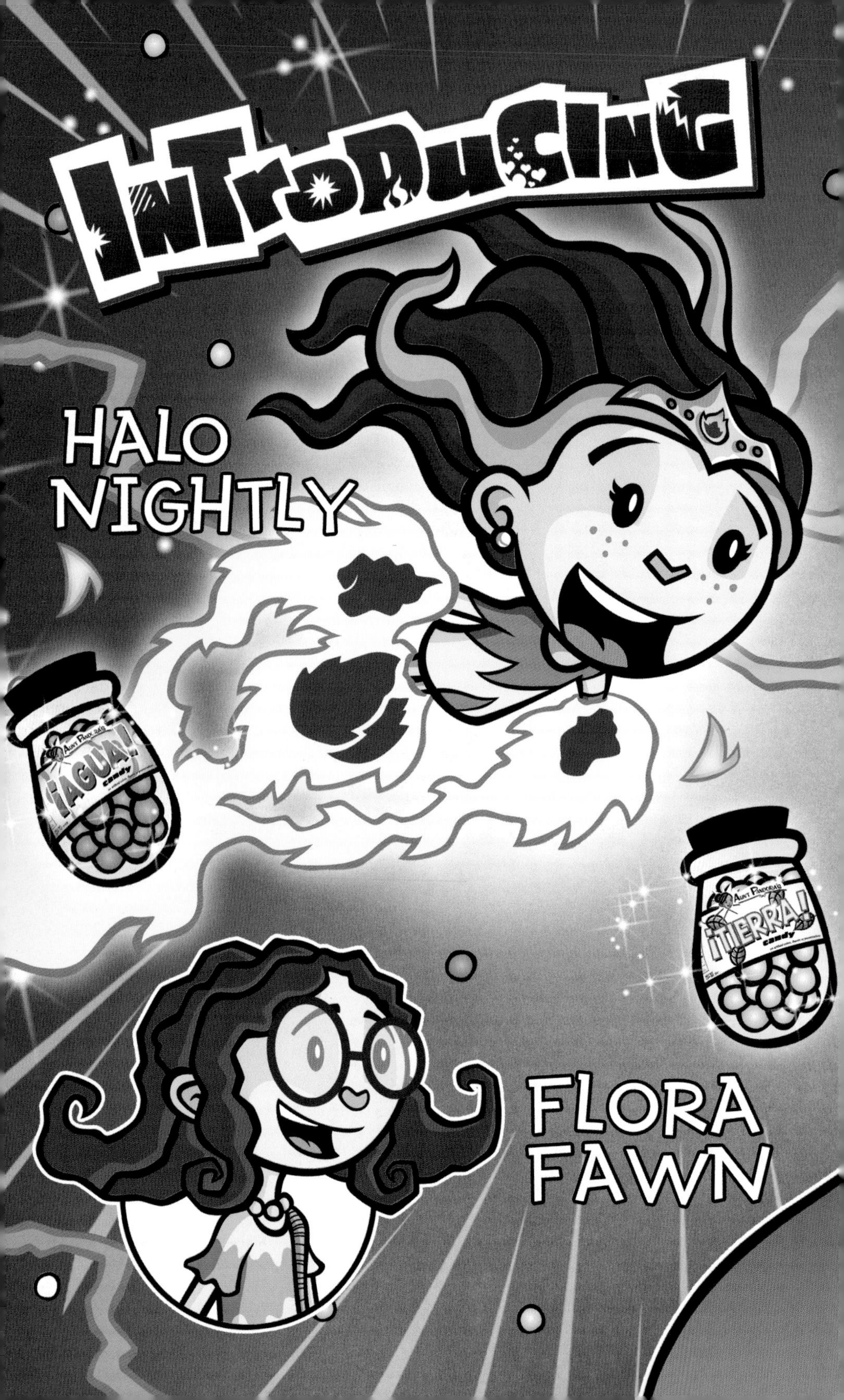
INTRODUCING
HALO NIGHTLY
¡AGUA! candy
¡TIERRA! candy
FLORA FAWN

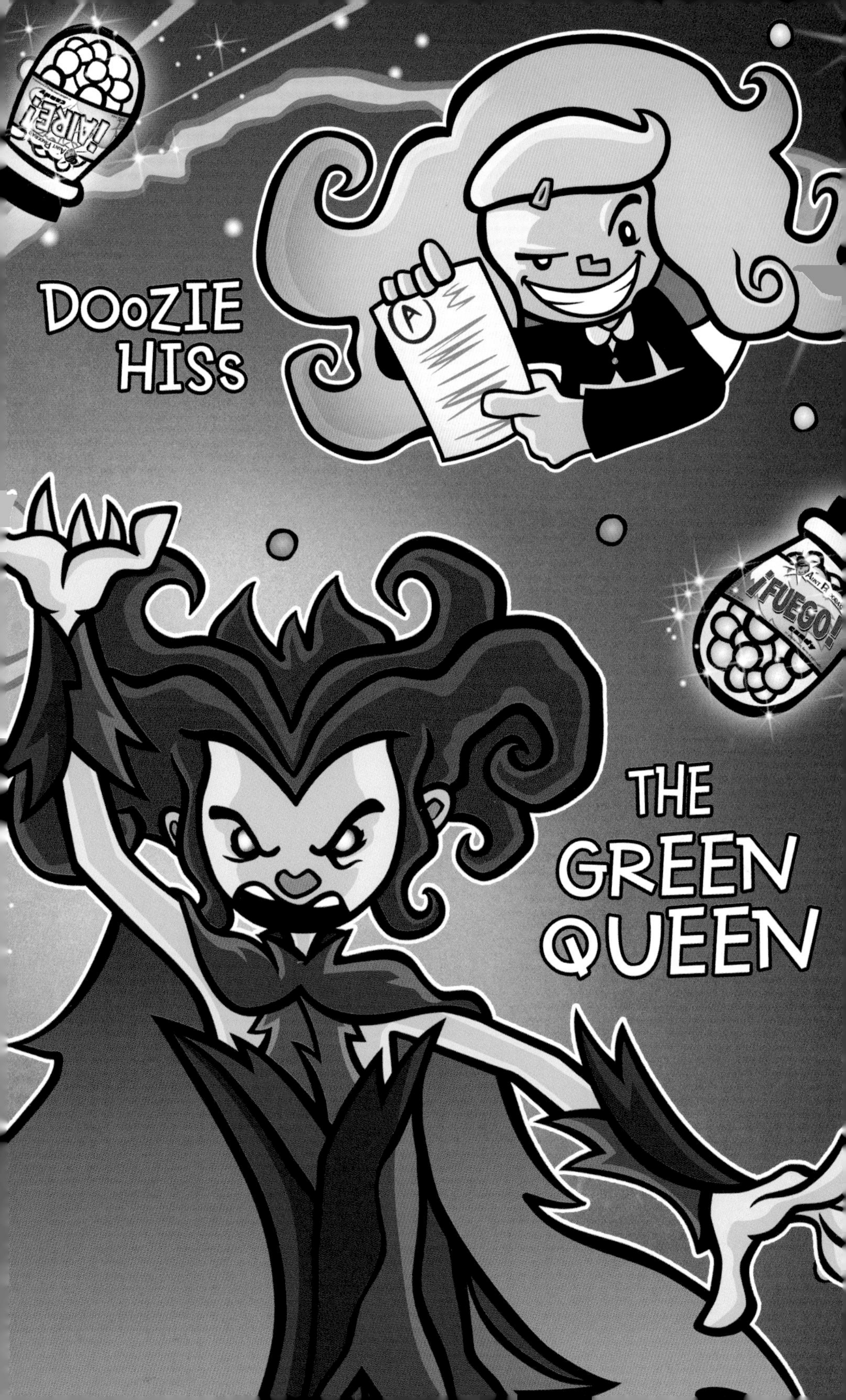
DOoZIE HISs
THE GREEN QUEEN
¡AIRE!
¡FUEGO!

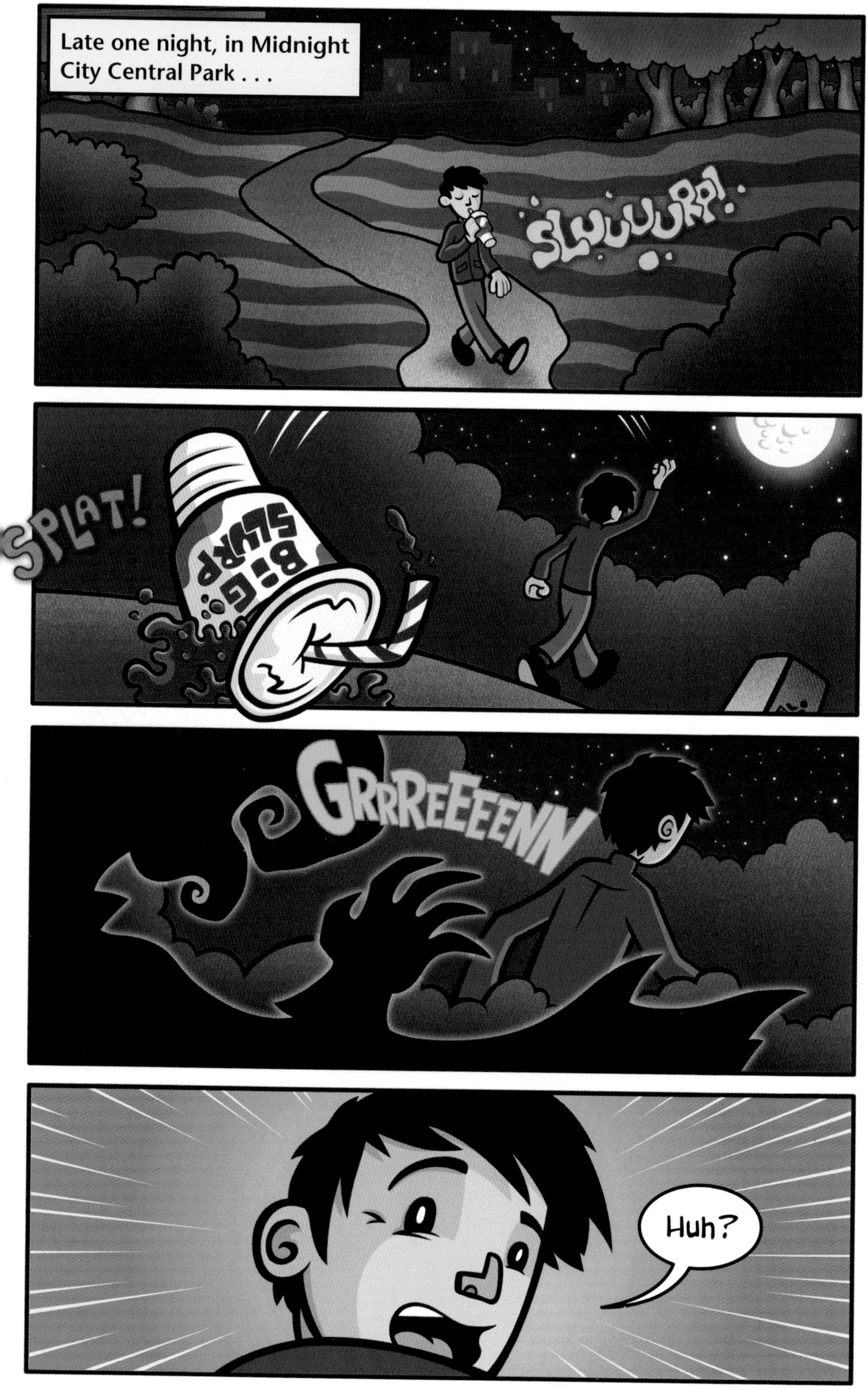
Late one night, in Midnight City Central Park . . .
SLUUUURP!
SPLAT!
BIG SLURP
GRRREEEENN
Huh?

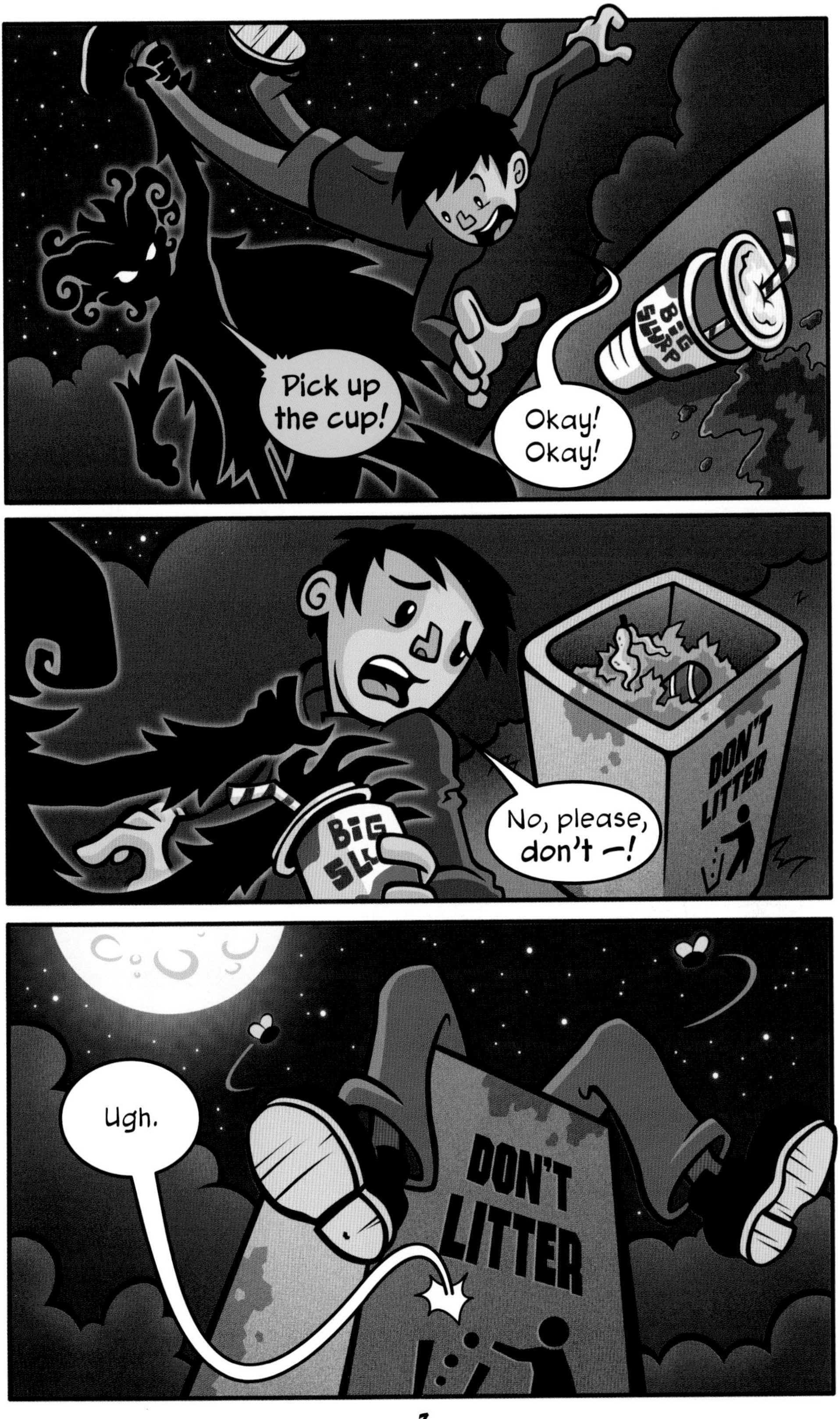
BIG SLURP
Pick up the cup!
Okay! Okay!
DON'T LITTER
BIG SL
No, please, don't —!
Ugh.
DON'T LITTER

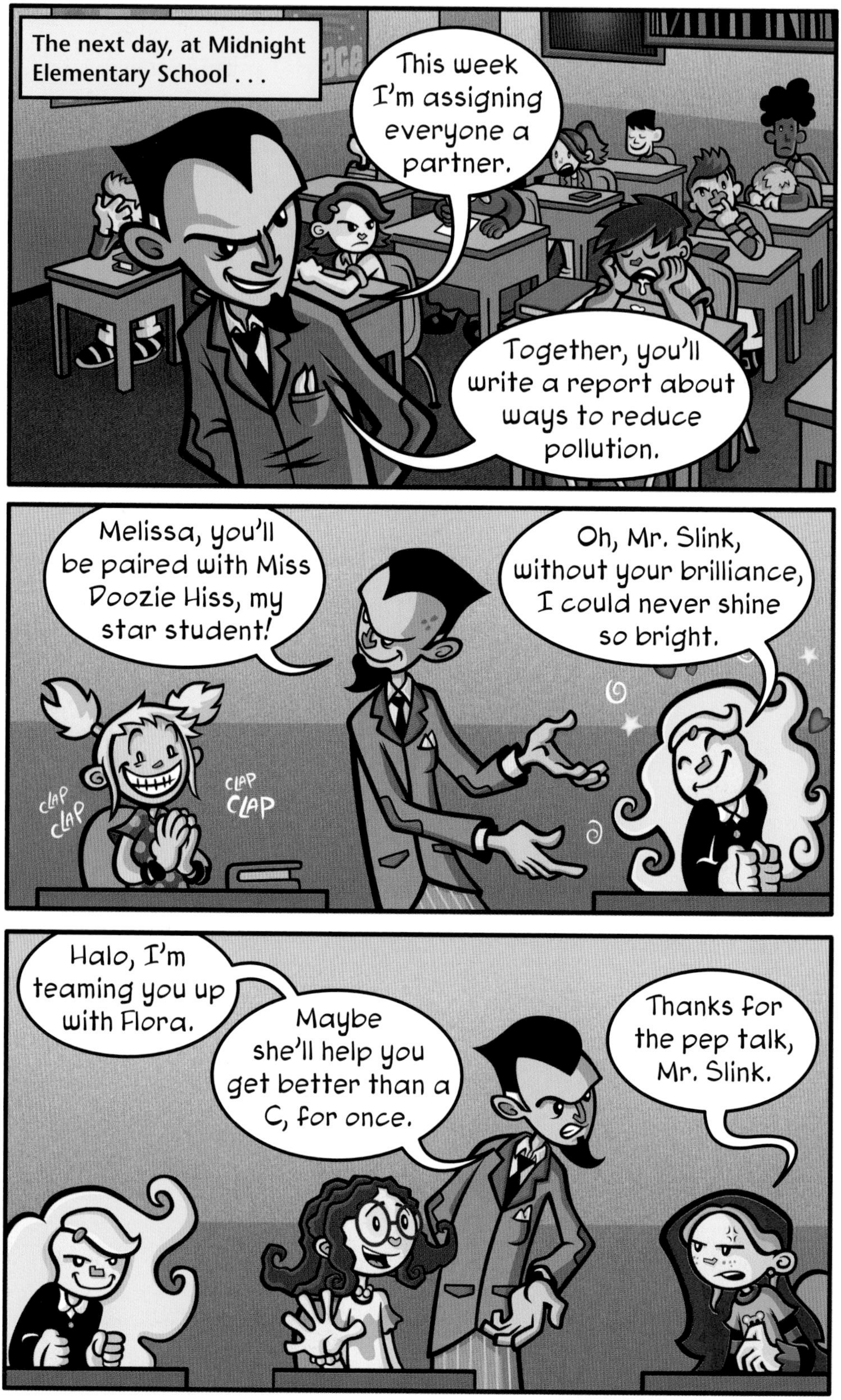
The next day, at Midnight Elementary School . . .
This week I'm assigning everyone a partner.
Together, you'll write a report about ways to reduce pollution.
Melissa, you'll be paired with Miss Doozie Hiss, my star student!
CLAP CLAP
CLAP CLAP
Oh, Mr. Slink, without your brilliance, I could never shine so bright.
Halo, I'm teaming you up with Flora.
Maybe she'll help you get better than a C, for once.
Thanks for the pep talk, Mr. Slink.

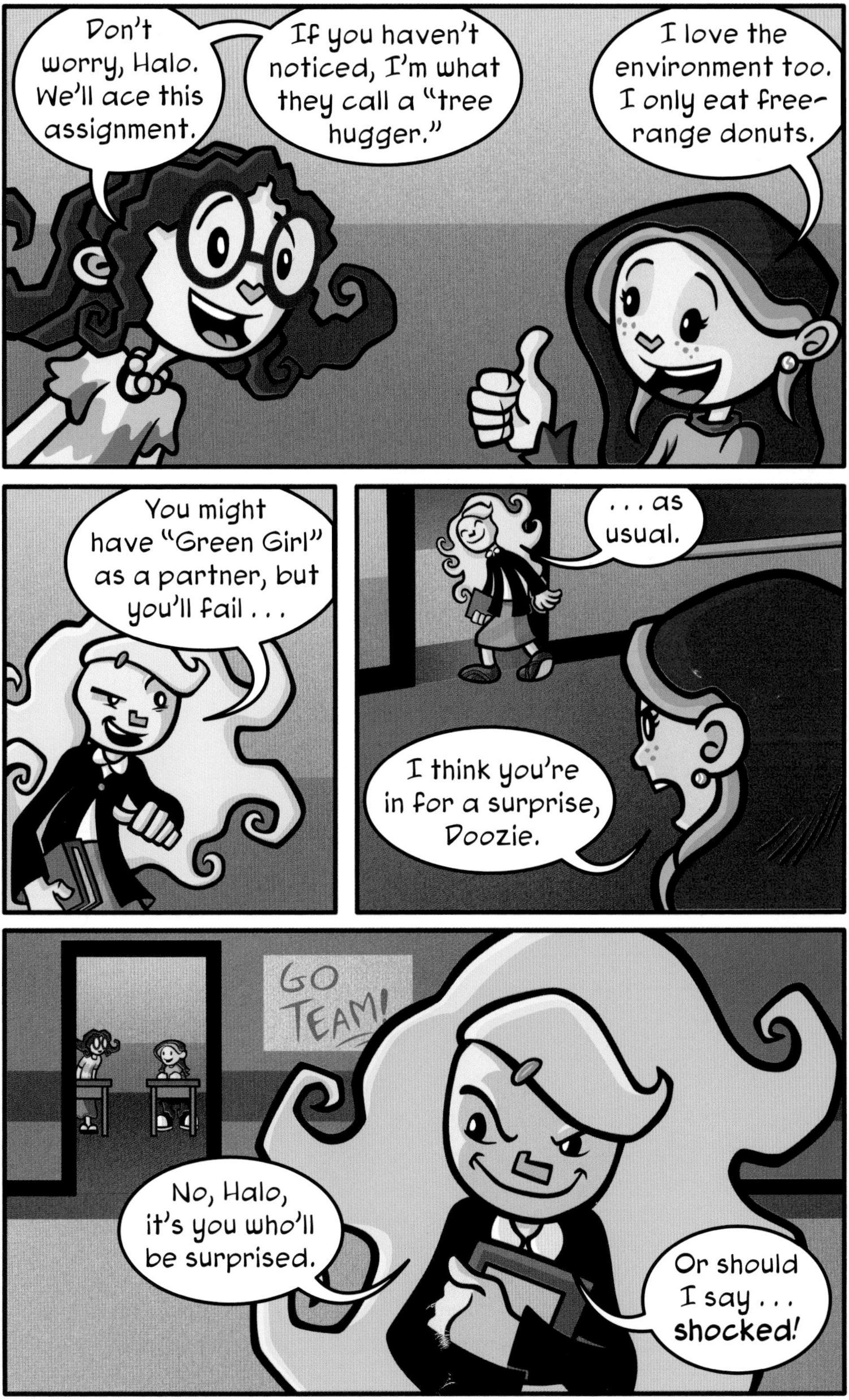
Don't worry, Halo. We'll ace this assignment.
If you haven't noticed, I'm what they call a "tree hugger."
I love the environment too. I only eat free-range donuts.
You might have "Green Girl" as a partner, but you'll fail . . .
. . . as usual.
I think you're in for a surprise, Doozie.
GO TEAM!
No, Halo, it's you who'll be surprised.
Or should I say . . . shocked!

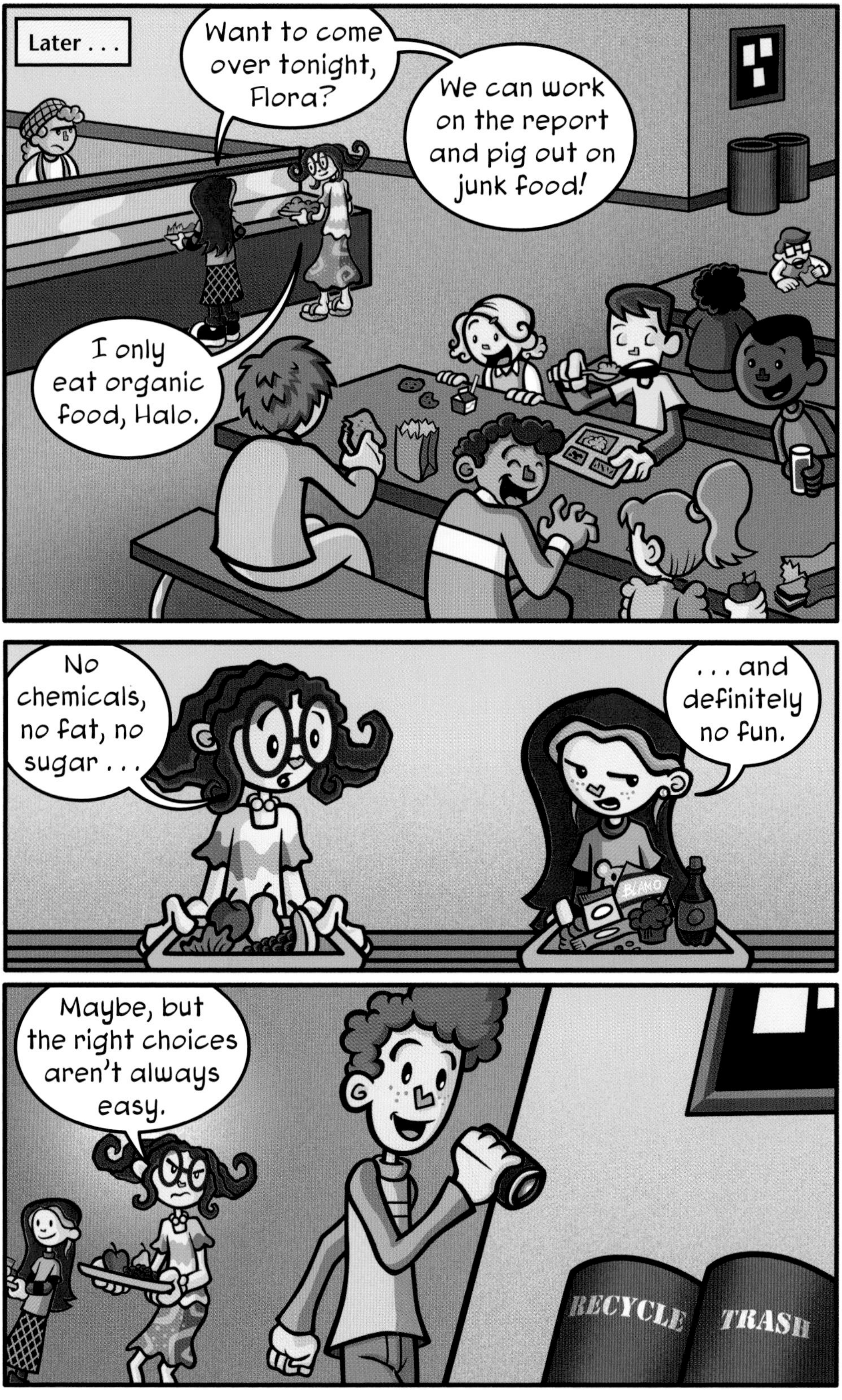
Later . . .
Want to come over tonight, Flora?
We can work on the report and pig out on junk food!
I only eat organic food, Halo.
No chemicals, no fat, no sugar . . .
. . . and definitely no fun.
BLAMO
Maybe, but the right choices aren't always easy.
RECYCLE
TRASH

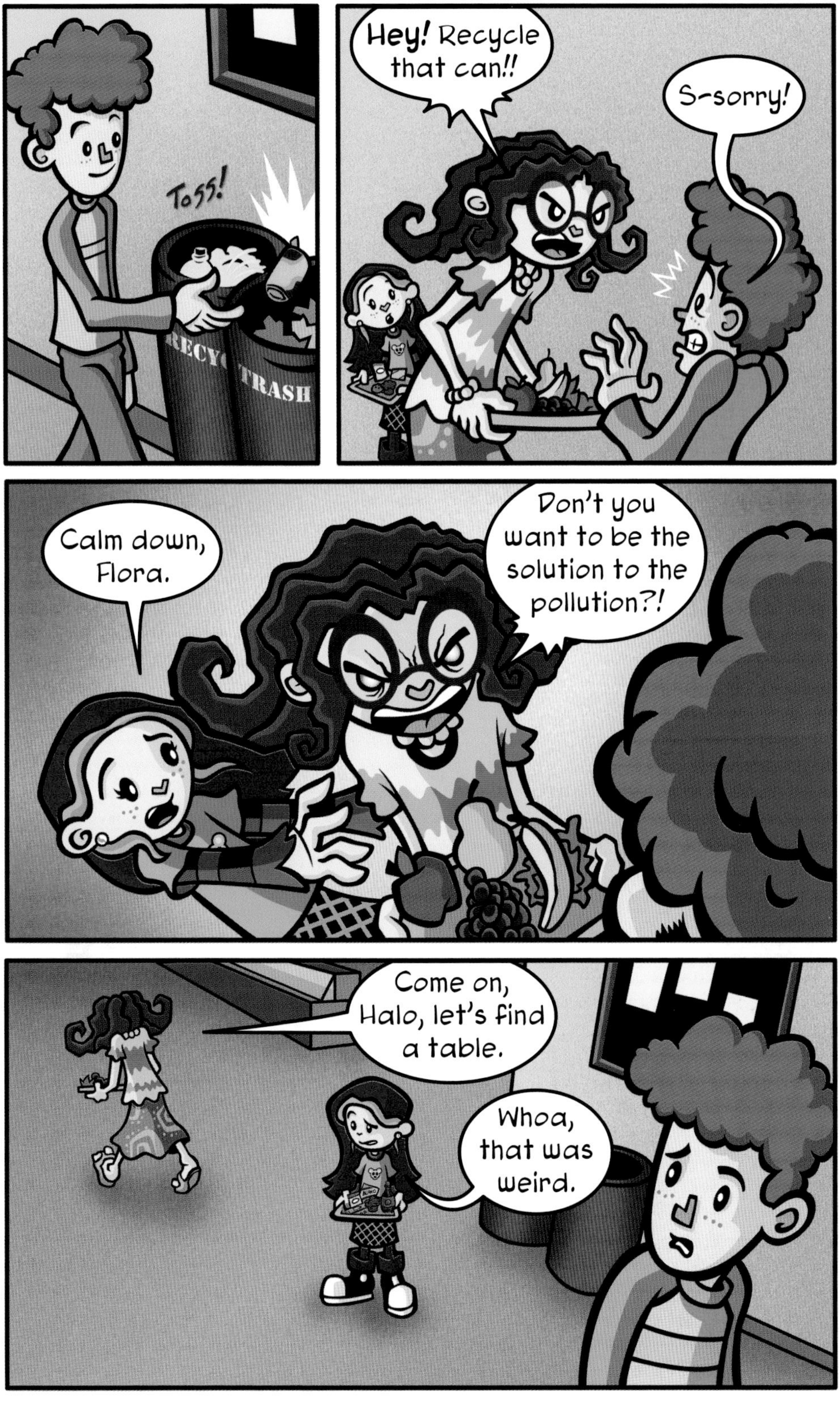
Toss!
RECYC
TRASH
Hey! Recycle that can!!
S-sorry!
Calm down, Flora.
Don't you want to be the solution to the pollution?!
Come on, Halo, let's find a table.
Whoa, that was weird.

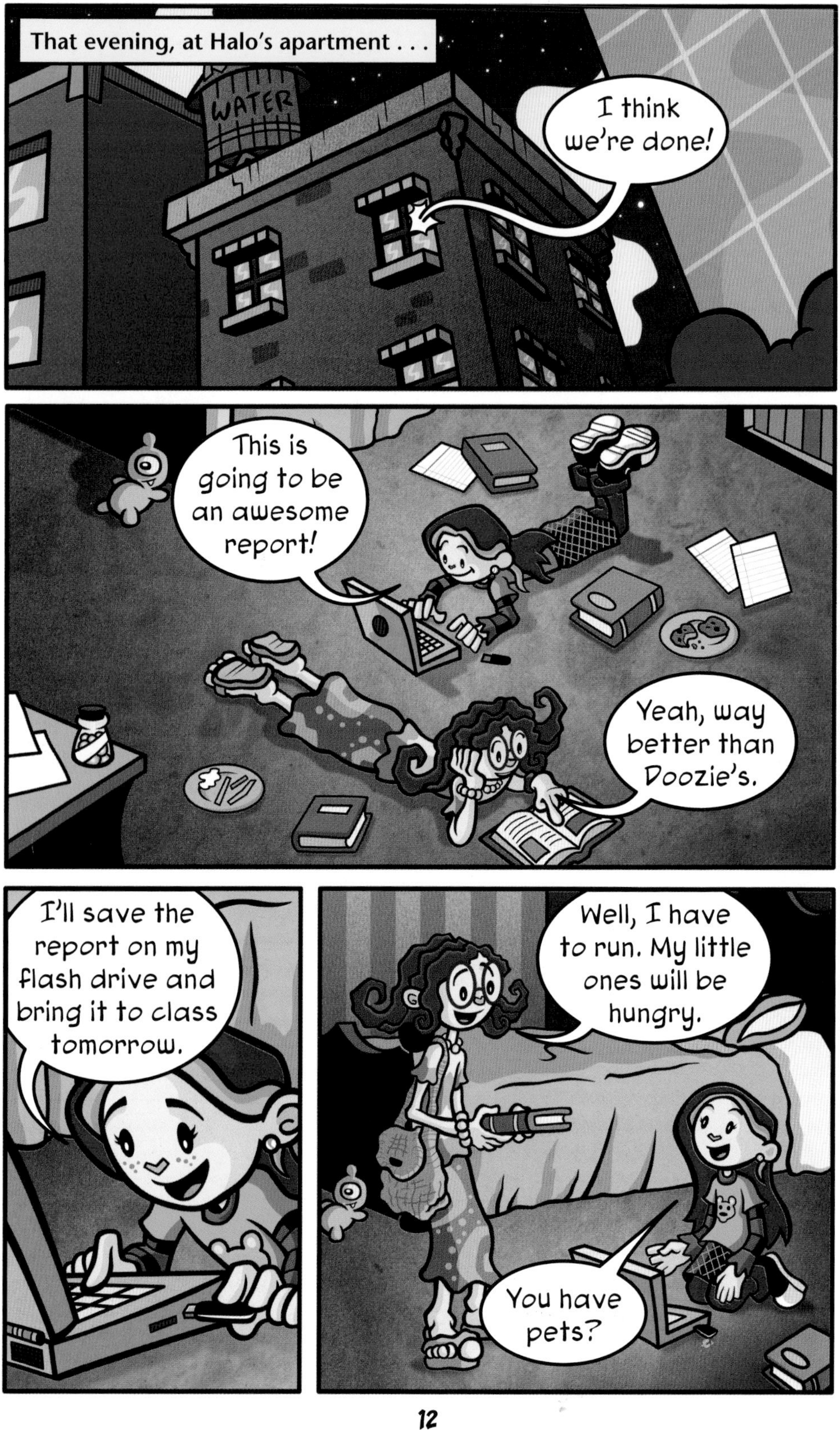
That evening, at Halo's apartment . . .
WATER
I think we're done!
This is going to be an awesome report!
Yeah, way better than Doozie's.
I'll save the report on my flash drive and bring it to class tomorrow.
Well, I have to run. My little ones will be hungry.
You have pets?

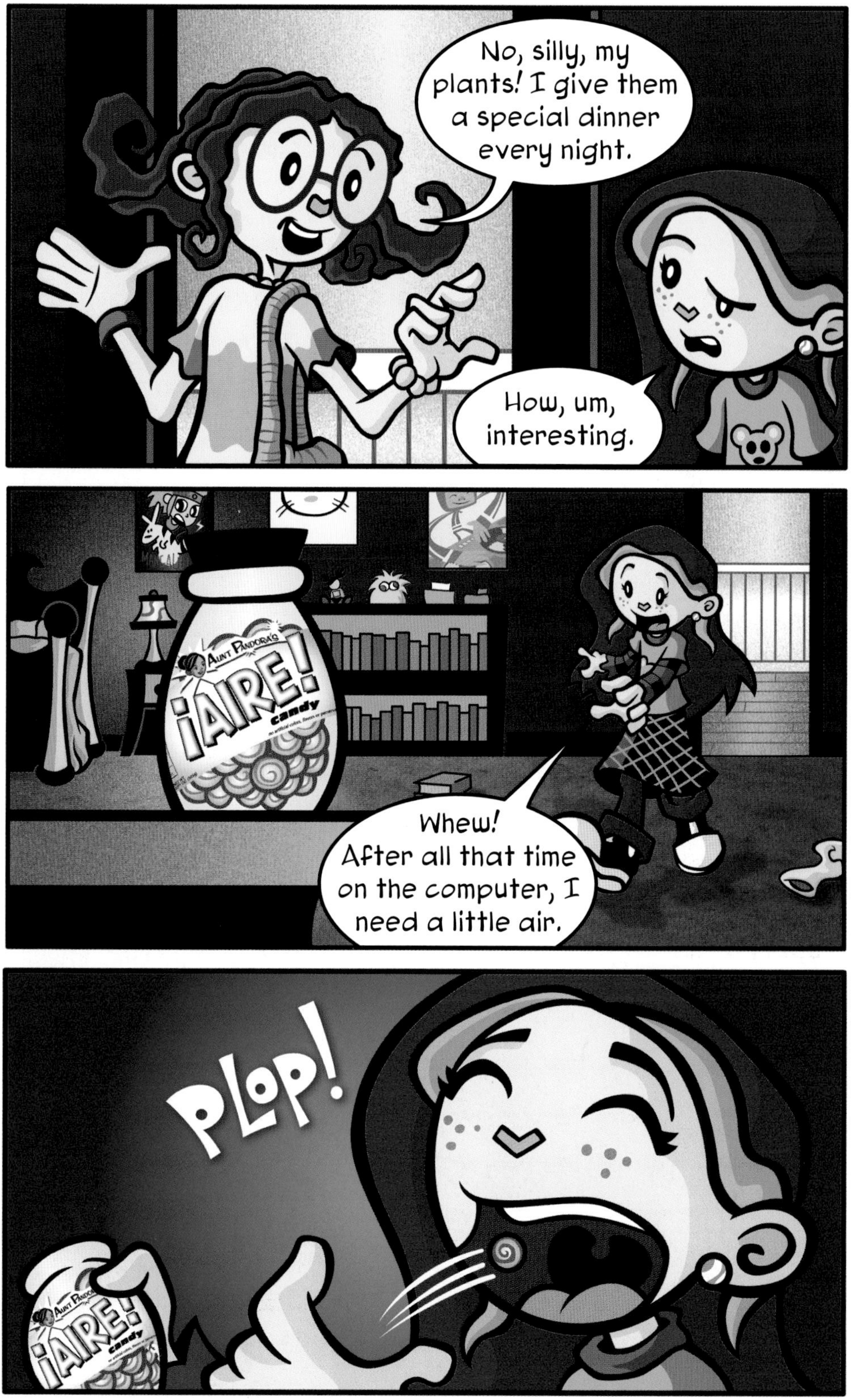
No, silly, my plants! I give them a special dinner every night.
How, um, interesting.
AUNT PANDORA'S
¡AIRE!
candy
Whew! After all that time on the computer, I need a little air.
PLOP!
AUNT PANDORA'S
¡AIRE!
candy

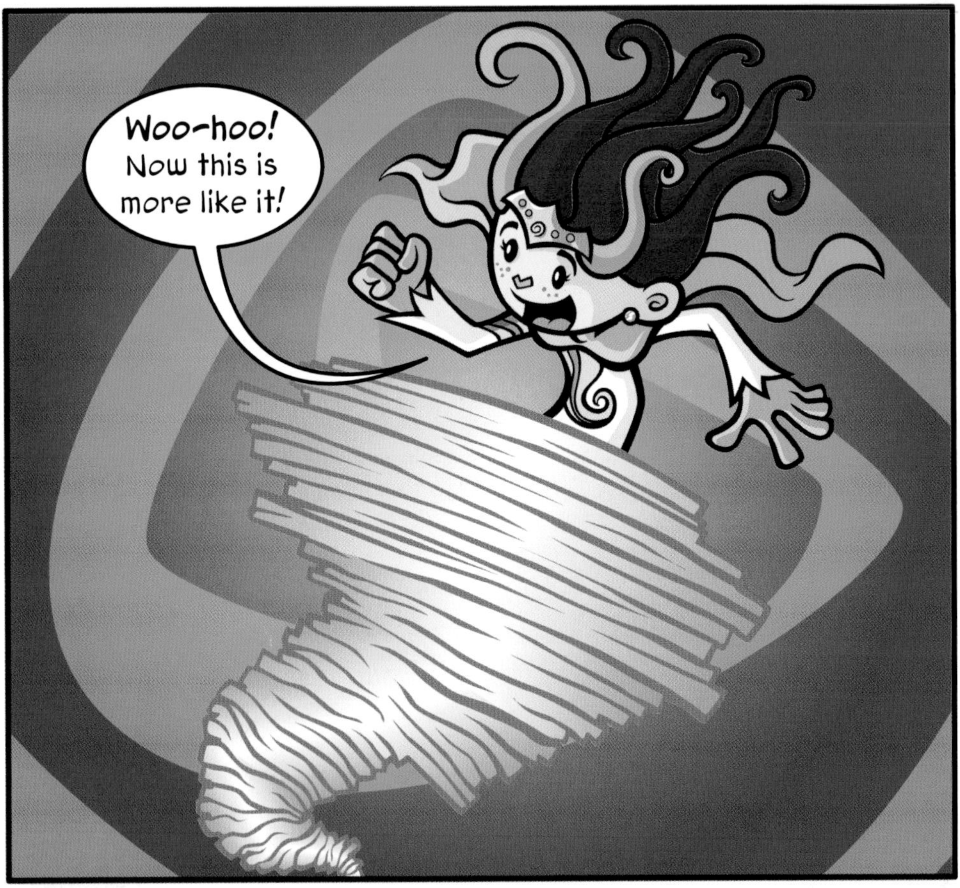
Woo-hoo! Now this is more like it!

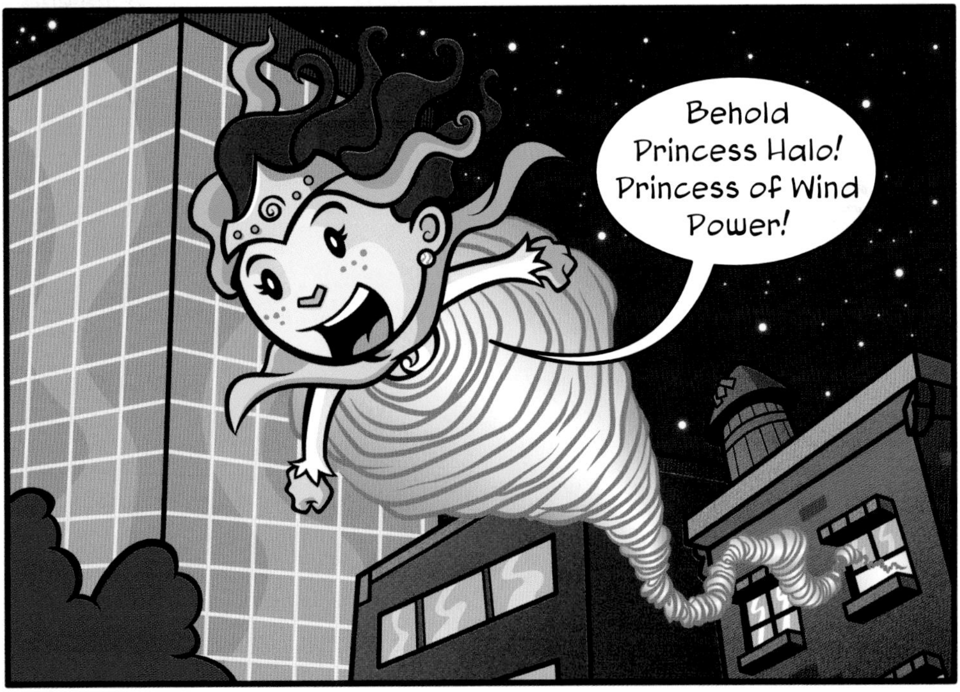
Behold Princess Halo! Princess of Wind Power!

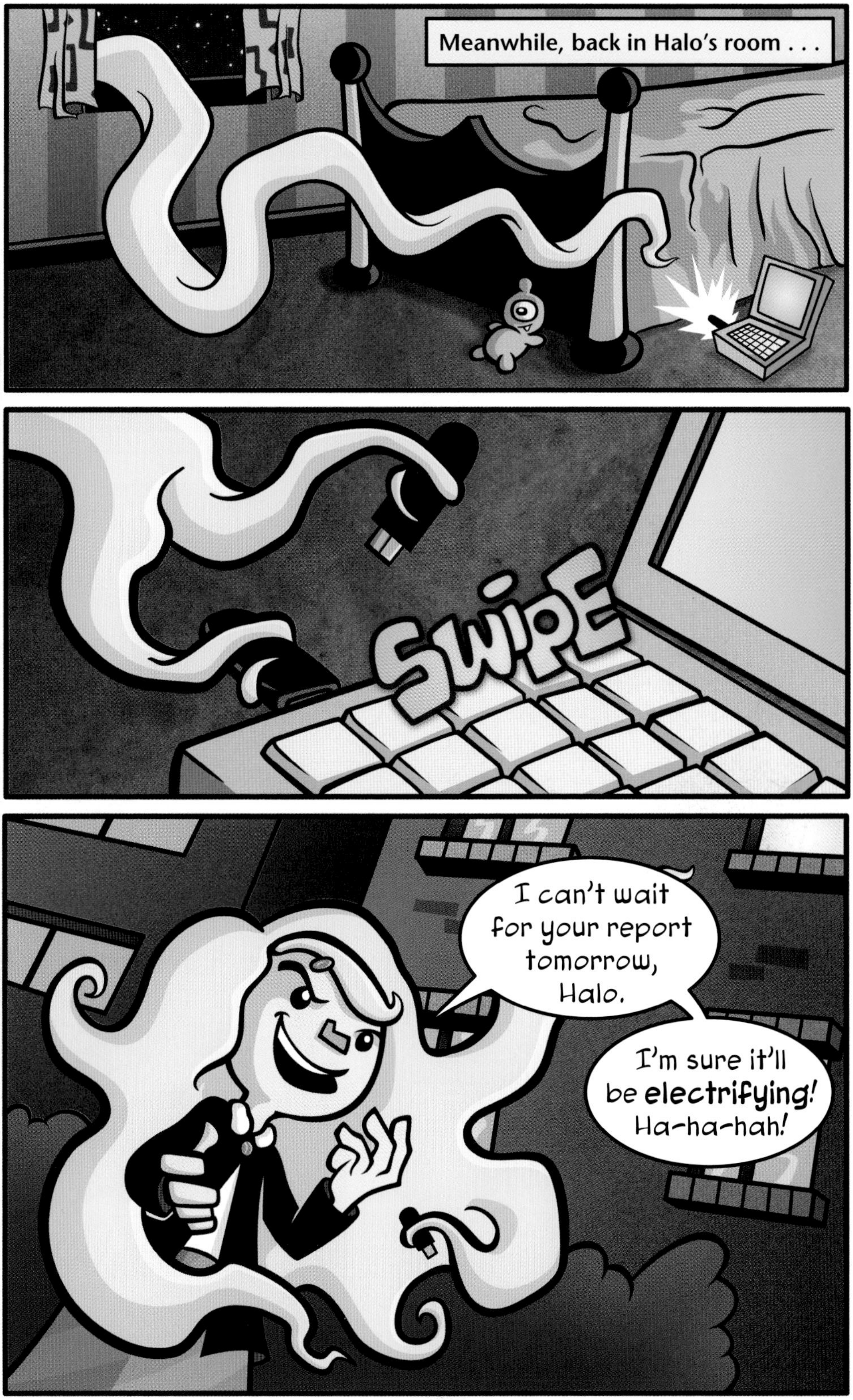
Meanwhile, back in Halo's room . . .
SWIPE
I can't wait for your report tomorrow, Halo.
I'm sure it'll be **electrifying**! Ha-ha-hah!

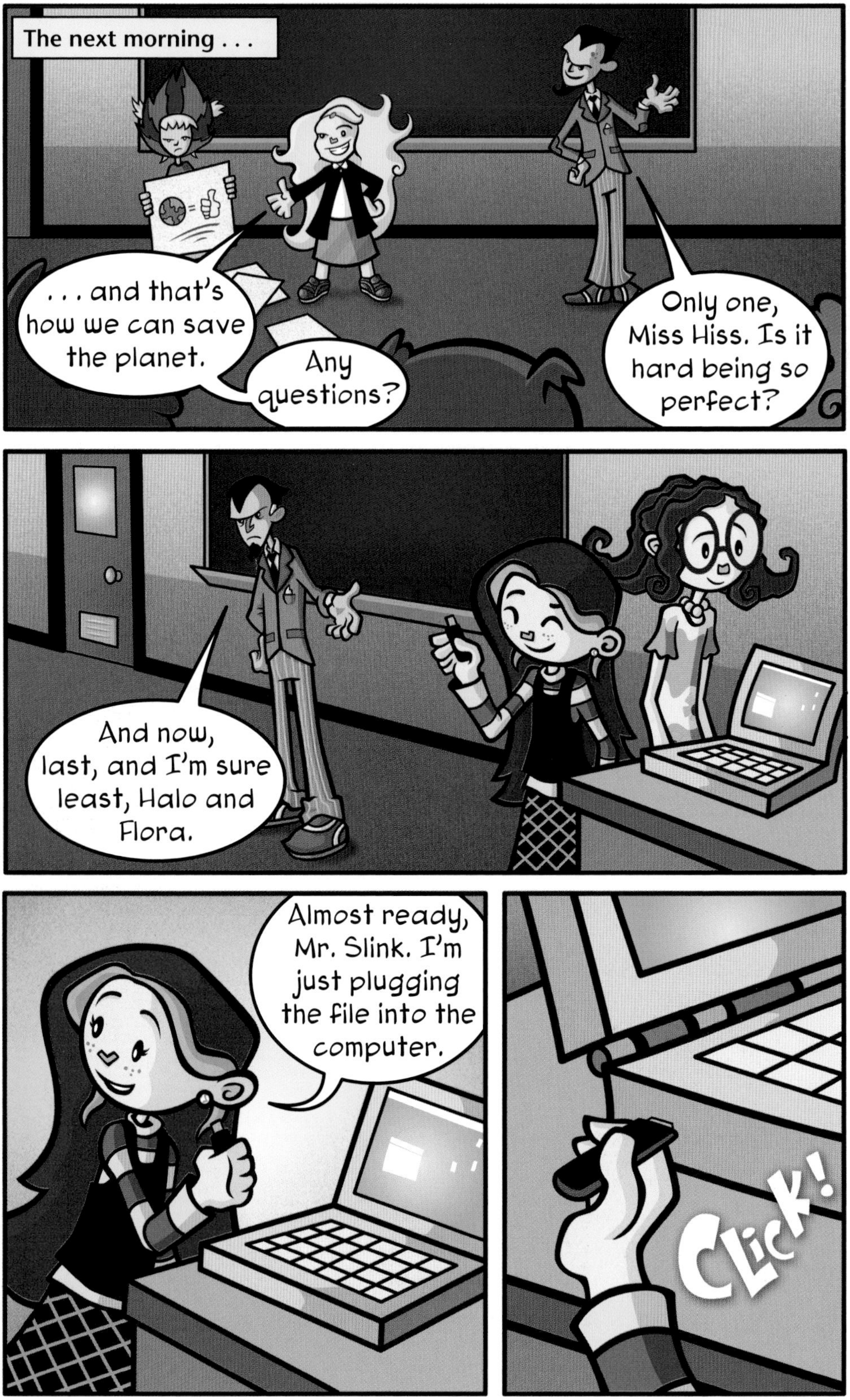
The next morning . . .
. . . and that's how we can save the planet.
Any questions?
Only one, Miss Hiss. Is it hard being so perfect?
And now, last, and I'm sure least, Halo and Flora.
Almost ready, Mr. Slink. I'm just plugging the file into the computer.
CLICK!

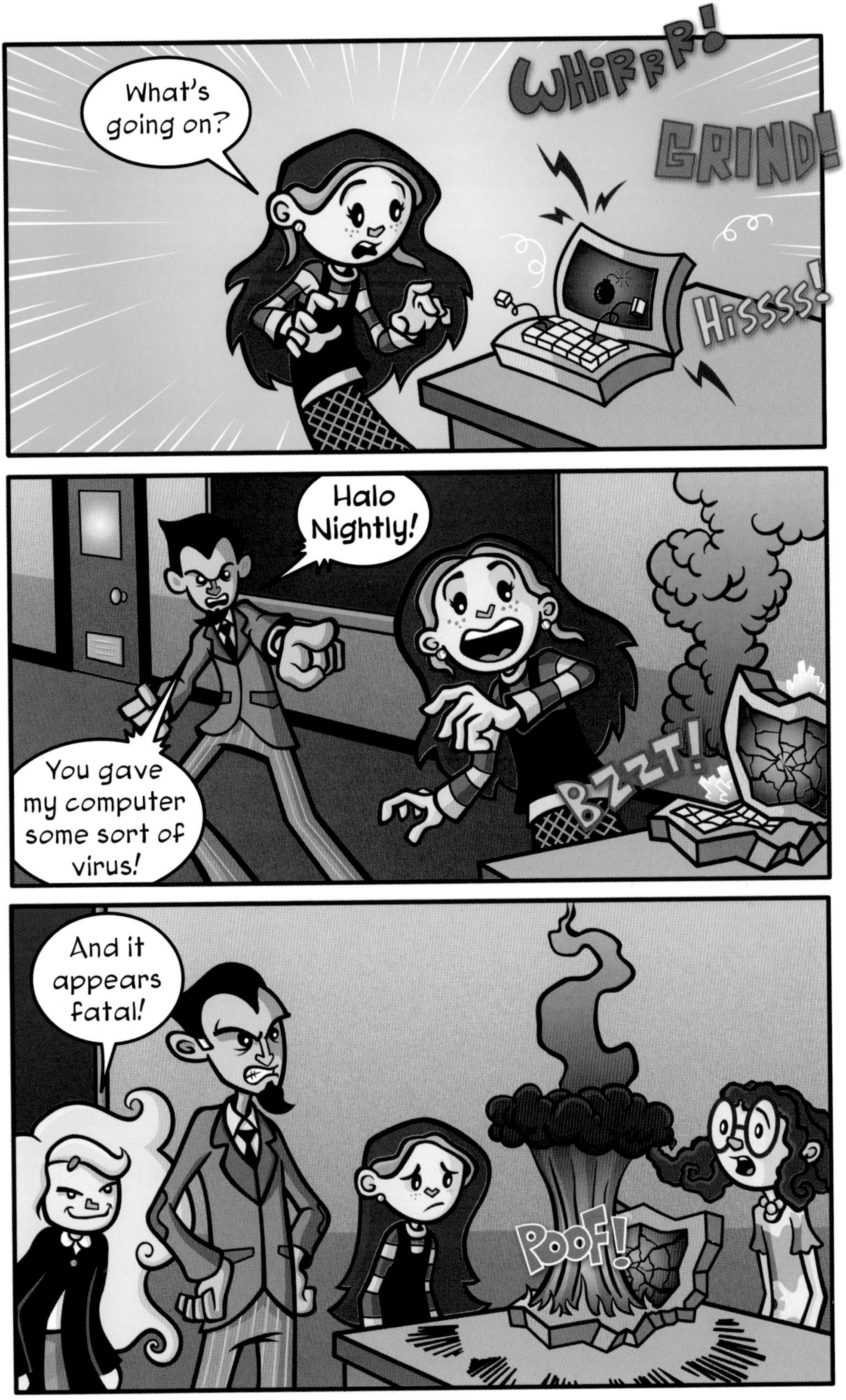
What's going on?
WHIRRR!
GRIND!
HISSSS!
Halo Nightly!
You gave my computer some sort of virus!
BZZZT!
And it appears fatal!
POOF!

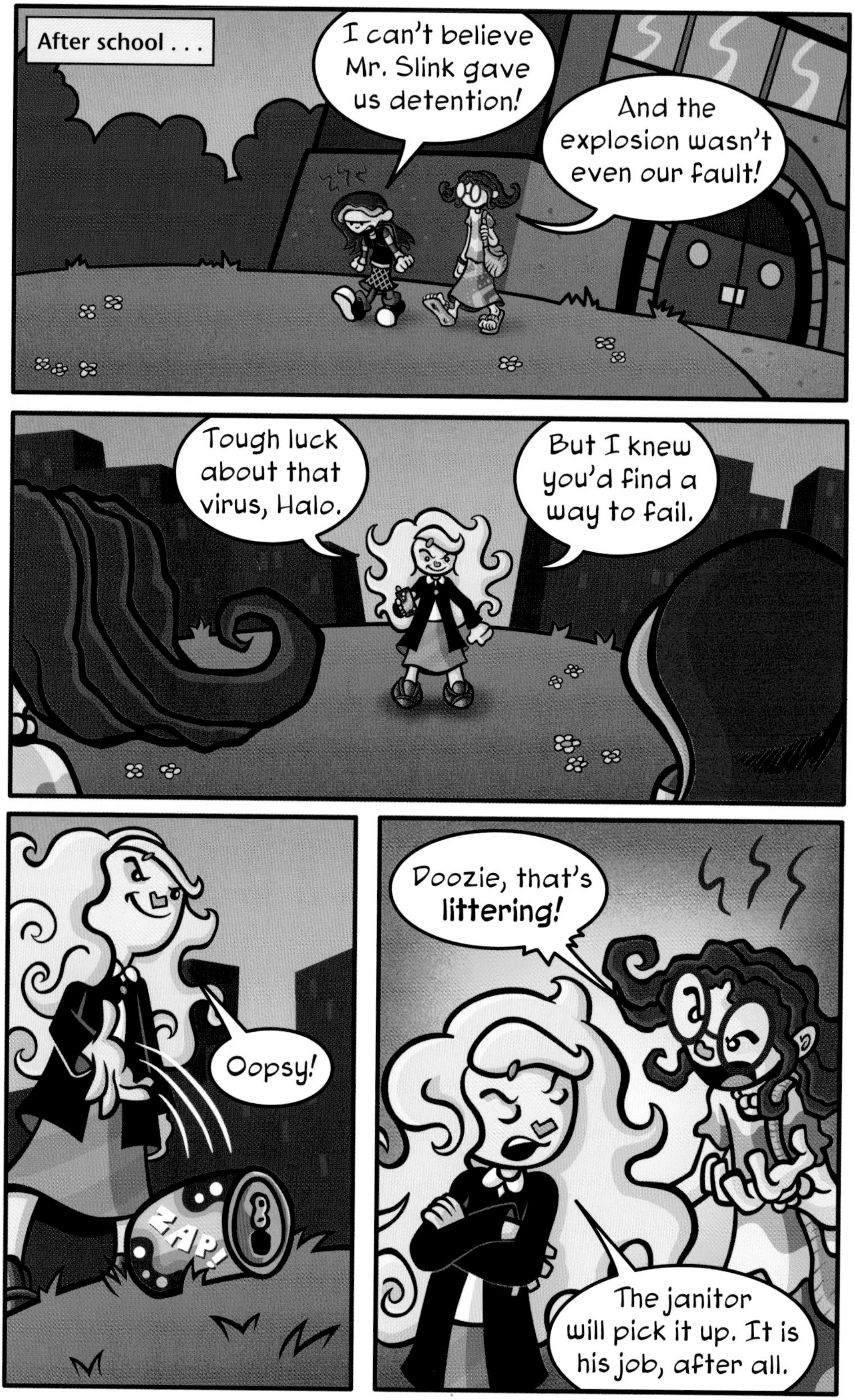
After school . . .
I can't believe Mr. Slink gave us detention!
And the explosion wasn't even our fault!
Tough luck about that virus, Halo.
But I knew you'd find a way to fail.
Oopsy!
ZAP!
Doozie, that's **littering!**
The janitor will pick it up. It is his job, after all.

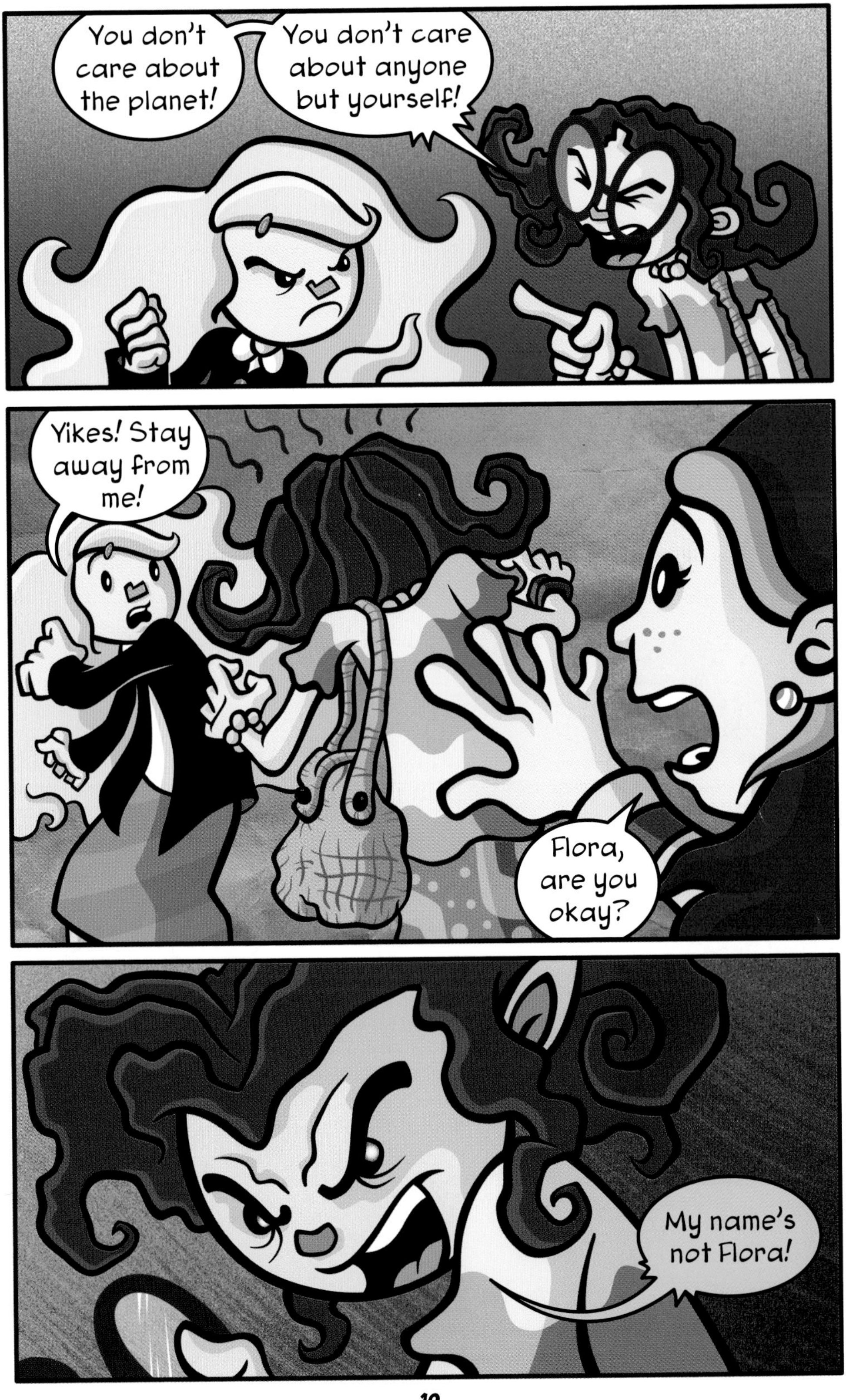
You don't care about the planet!
You don't care about anyone but yourself!
Yikes! Stay away from me!
Flora, are you okay?
My name's not Flora!

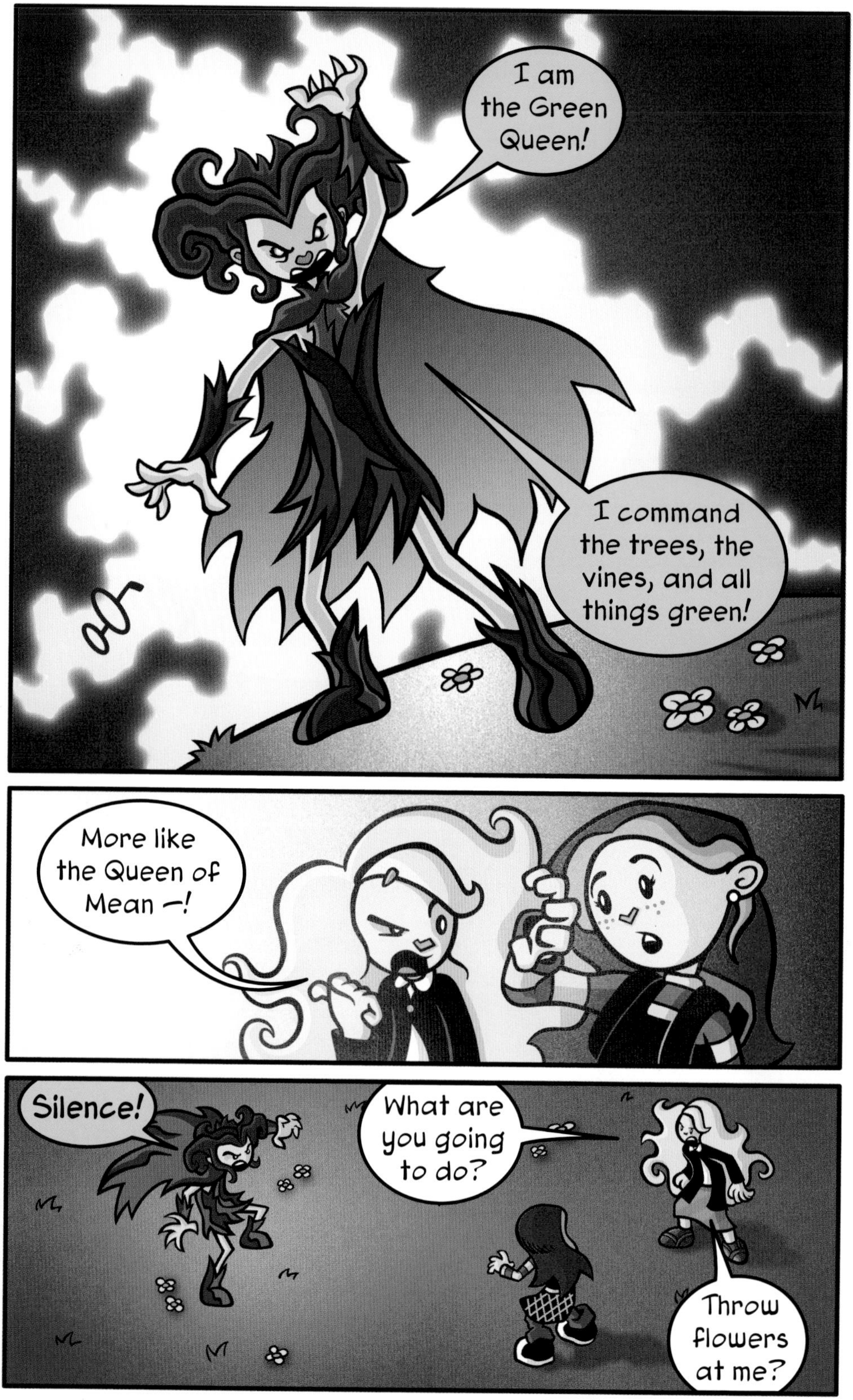
I am the Green Queen!
I command the trees, the vines, and all things green!
More like the Queen of Mean —!
Silence!
What are you going to do?
Throw flowers at me?

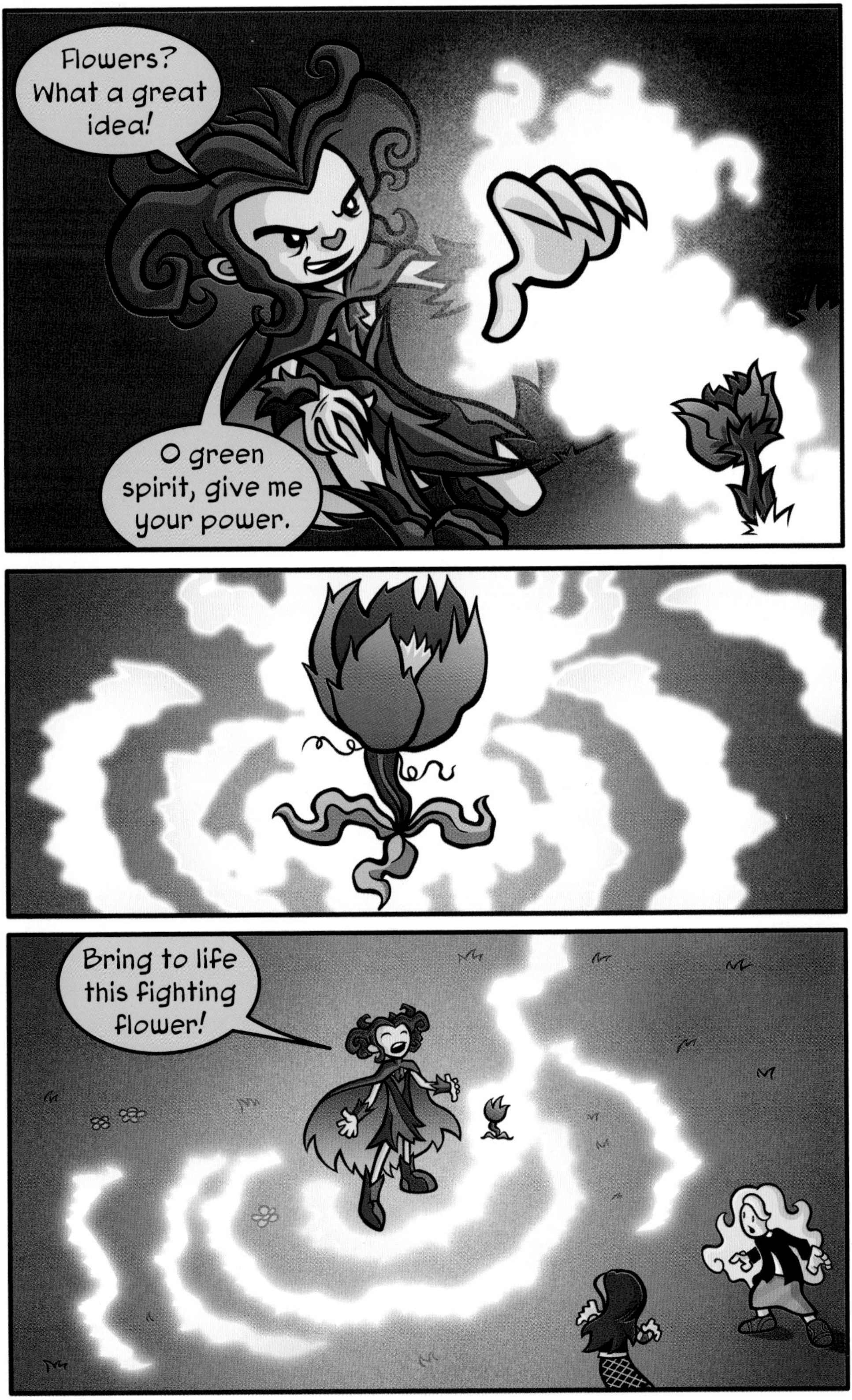
Flowers? What a great idea!
O green spirit, give me your power.
Bring to life this fighting flower!

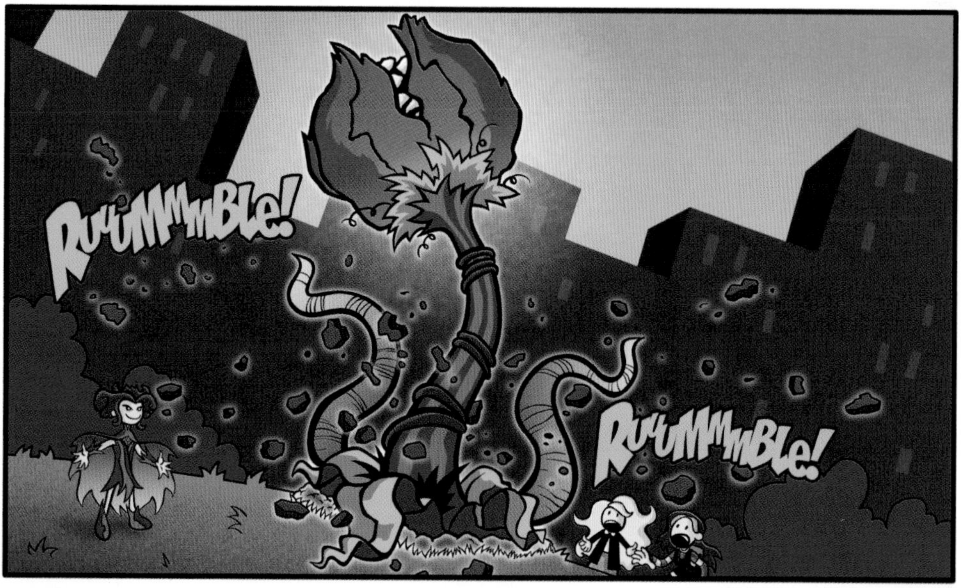
RUUMMMBLE!
RUUMMMBLE!

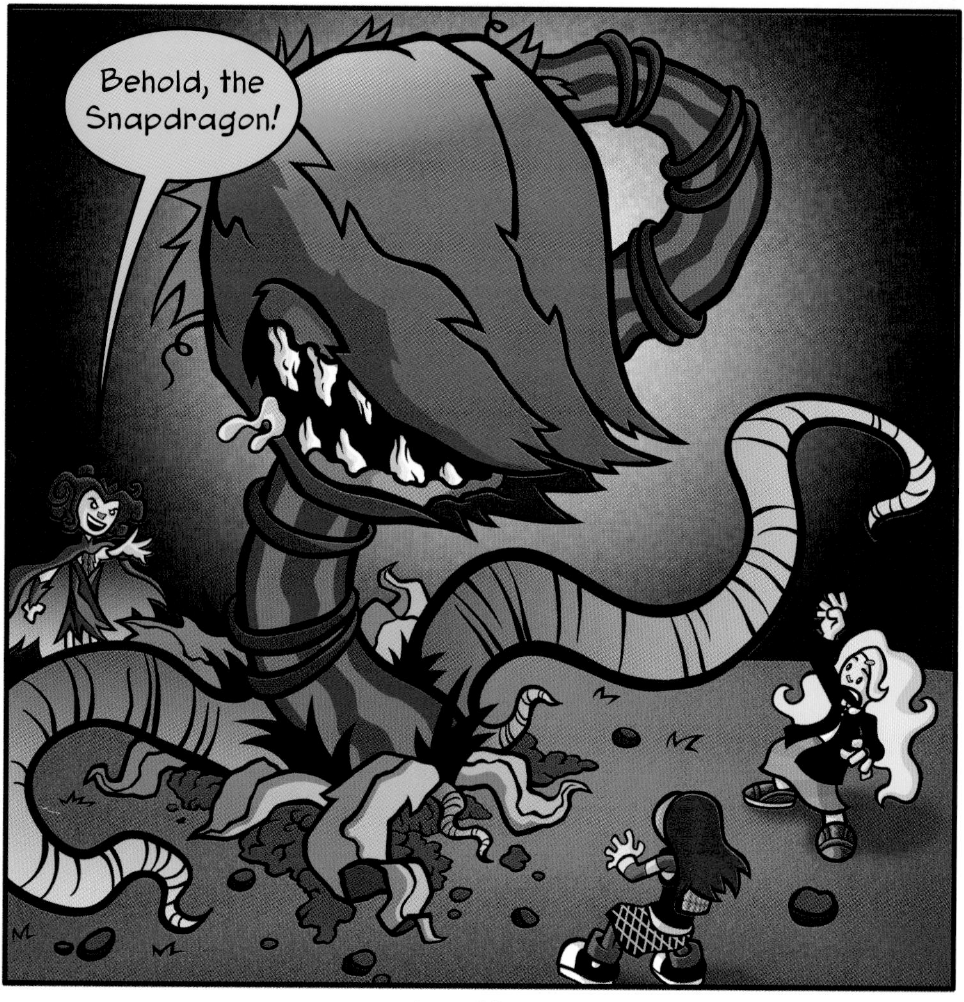
Behold, the Snapdragon!

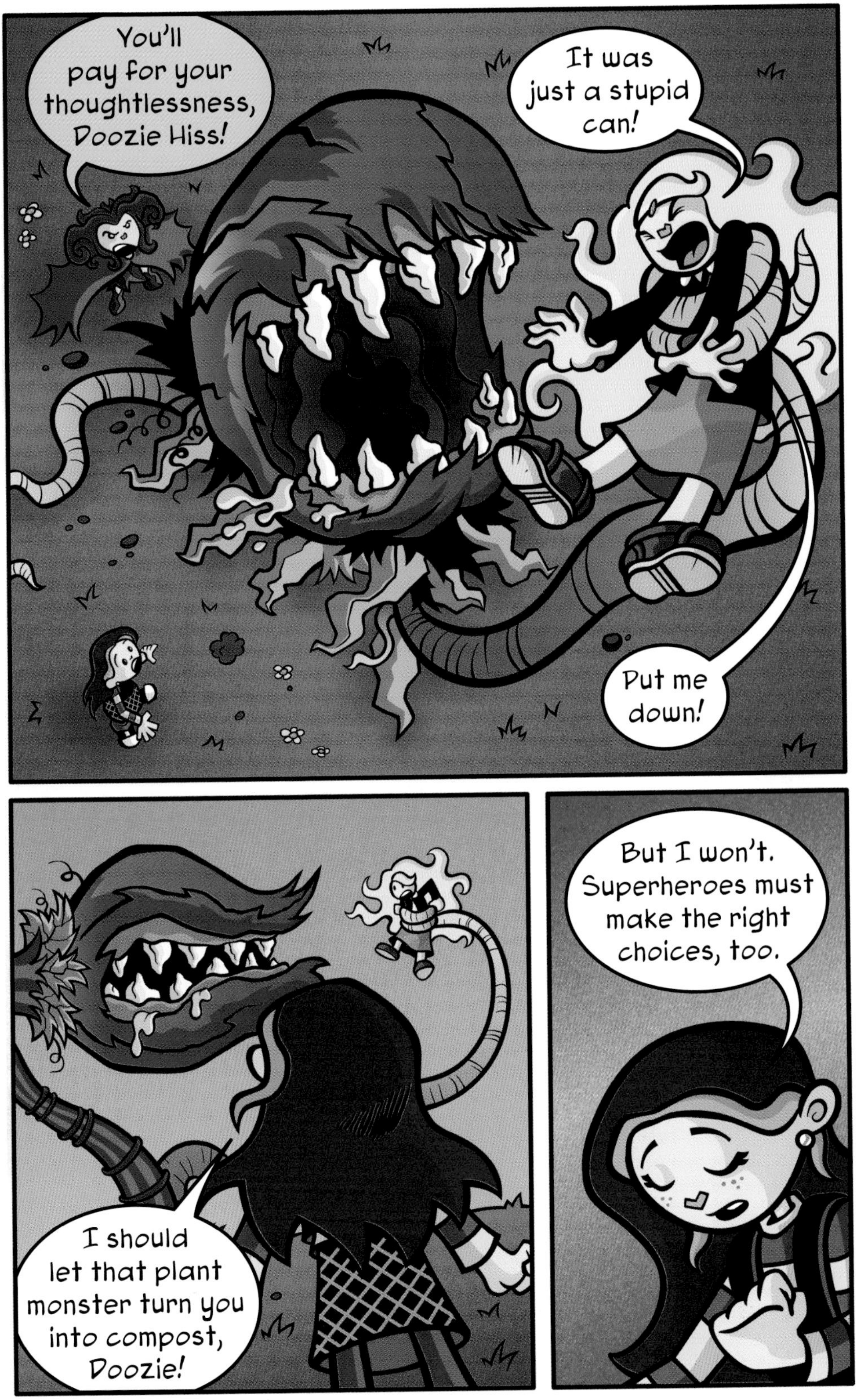
You'll pay for your thoughtlessness, Doozie Hiss!
It was just a stupid can!
Put me down!
I should let that plant monster turn you into compost, Doozie!
But I won't. Superheroes must make the right choices, too.

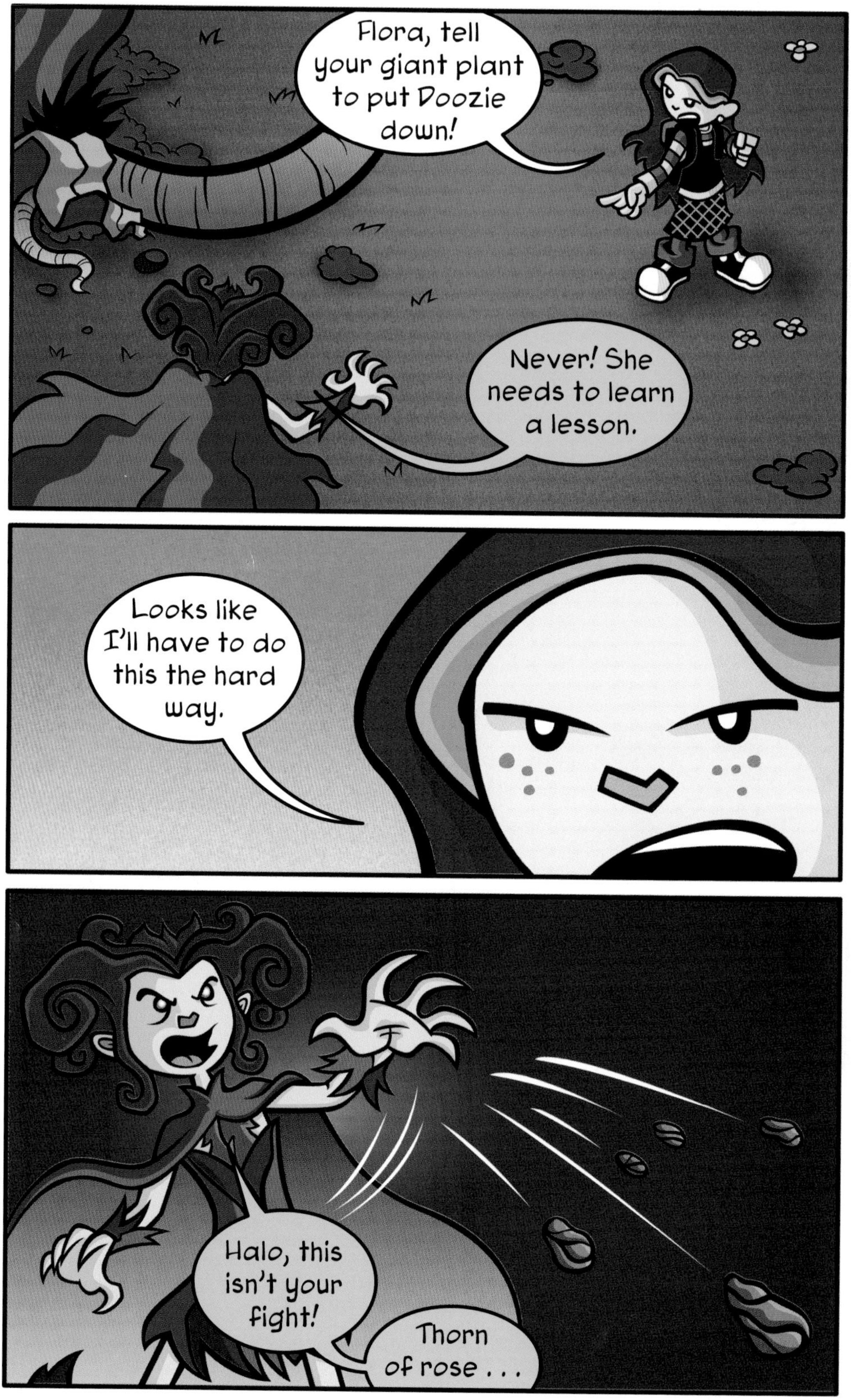
Flora, tell your giant plant to put Doozie down!
Never! She needs to learn a lesson.
Looks like I'll have to do this the hard way.
Halo, this isn't your fight!
Thorn of rose . . .

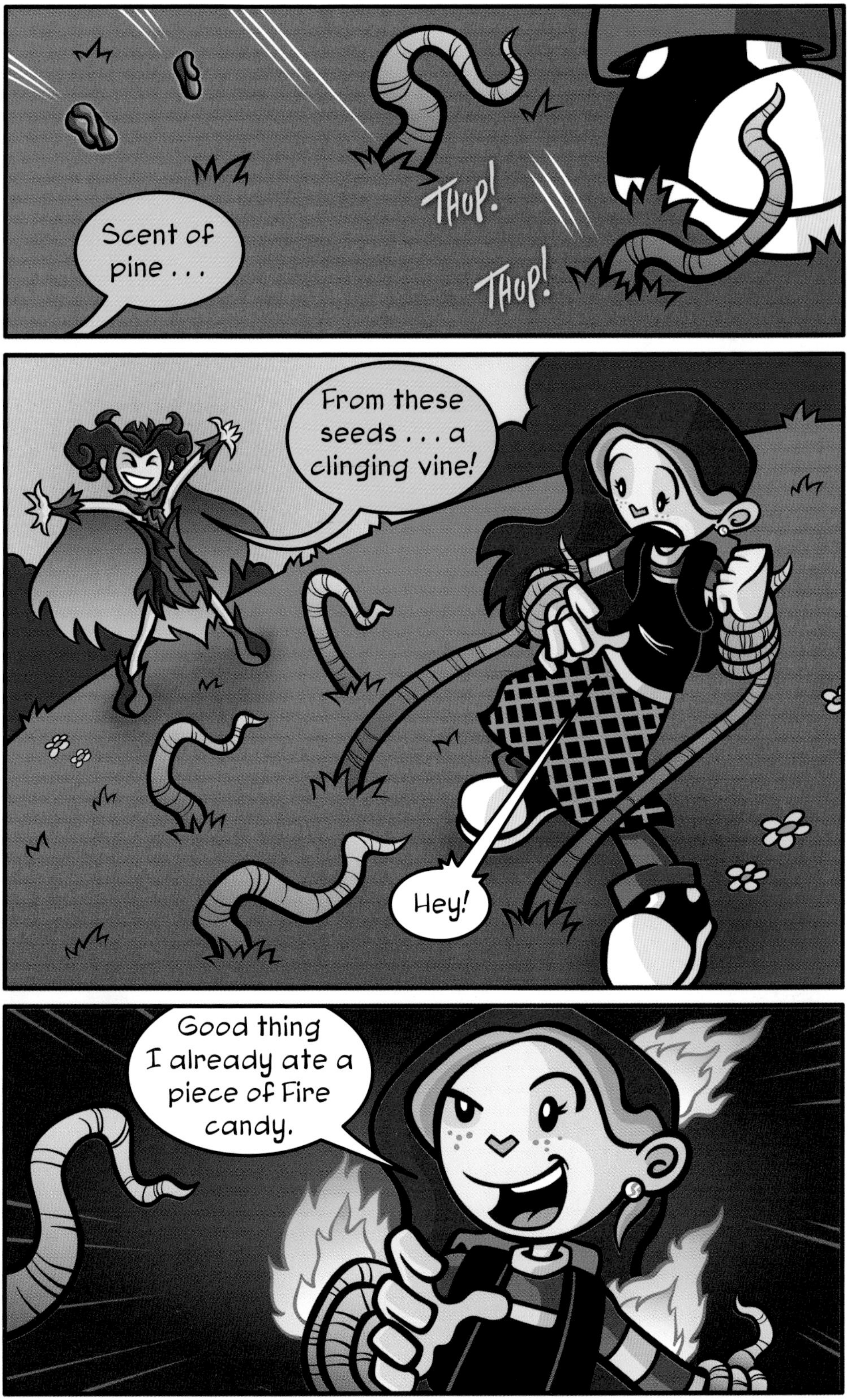
THUP!
THUP!
Scent of pine . . .
From these seeds . . . a clinging vine!
Hey!
Good thing I already ate a piece of Fire candy.

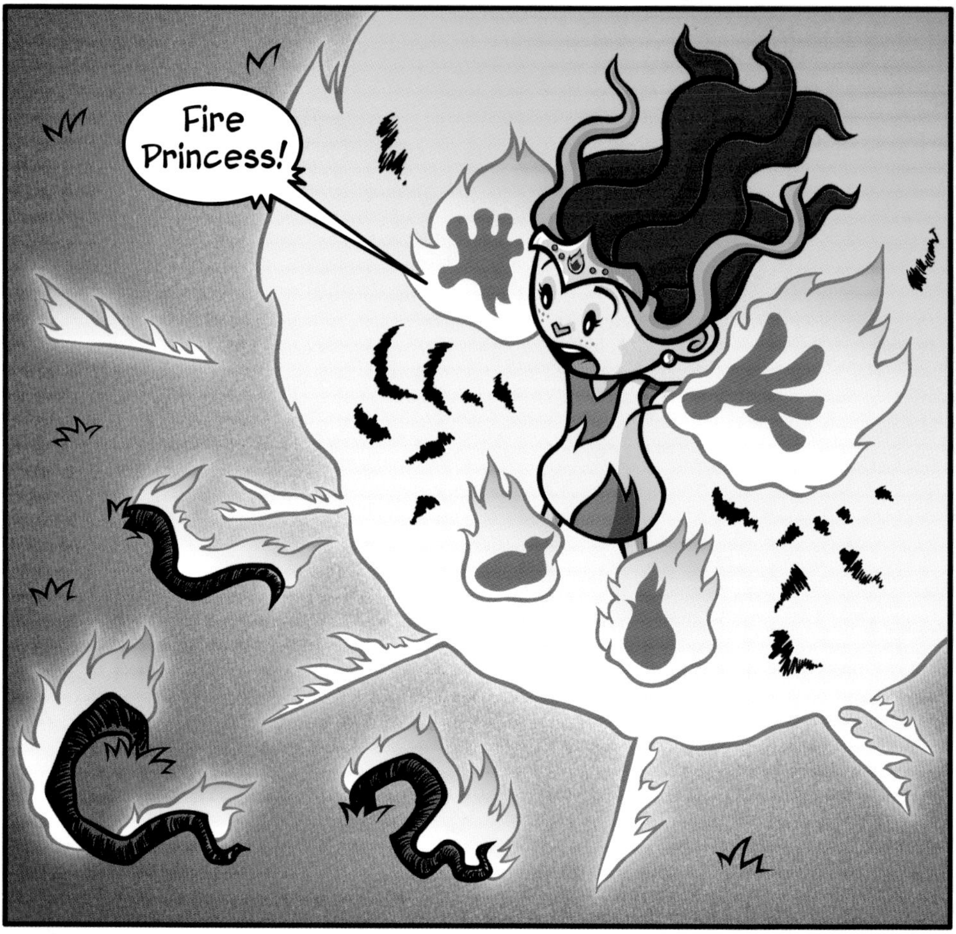
Fire
Princess!

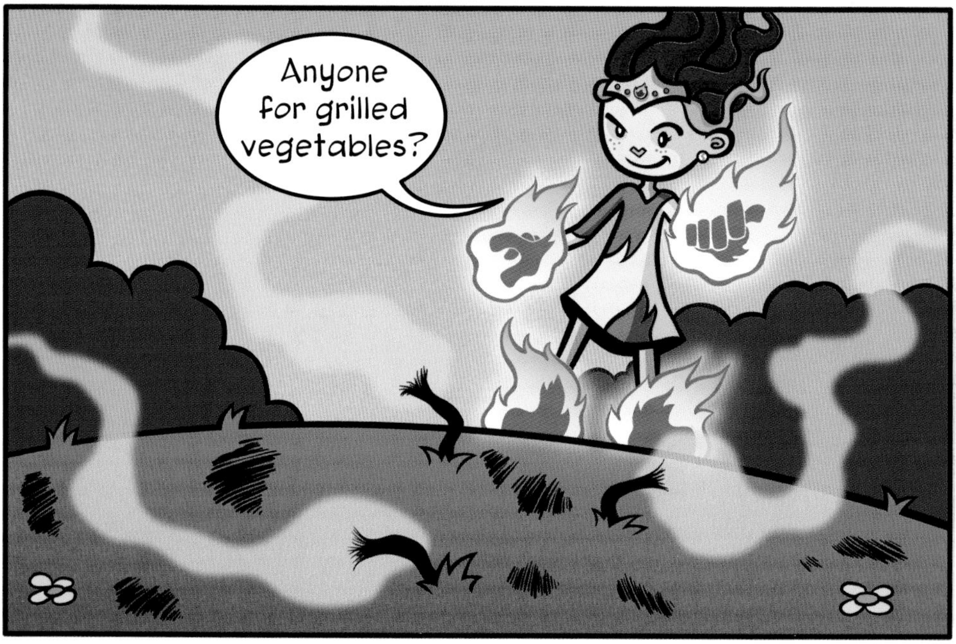
Anyone
for grilled
vegetables?

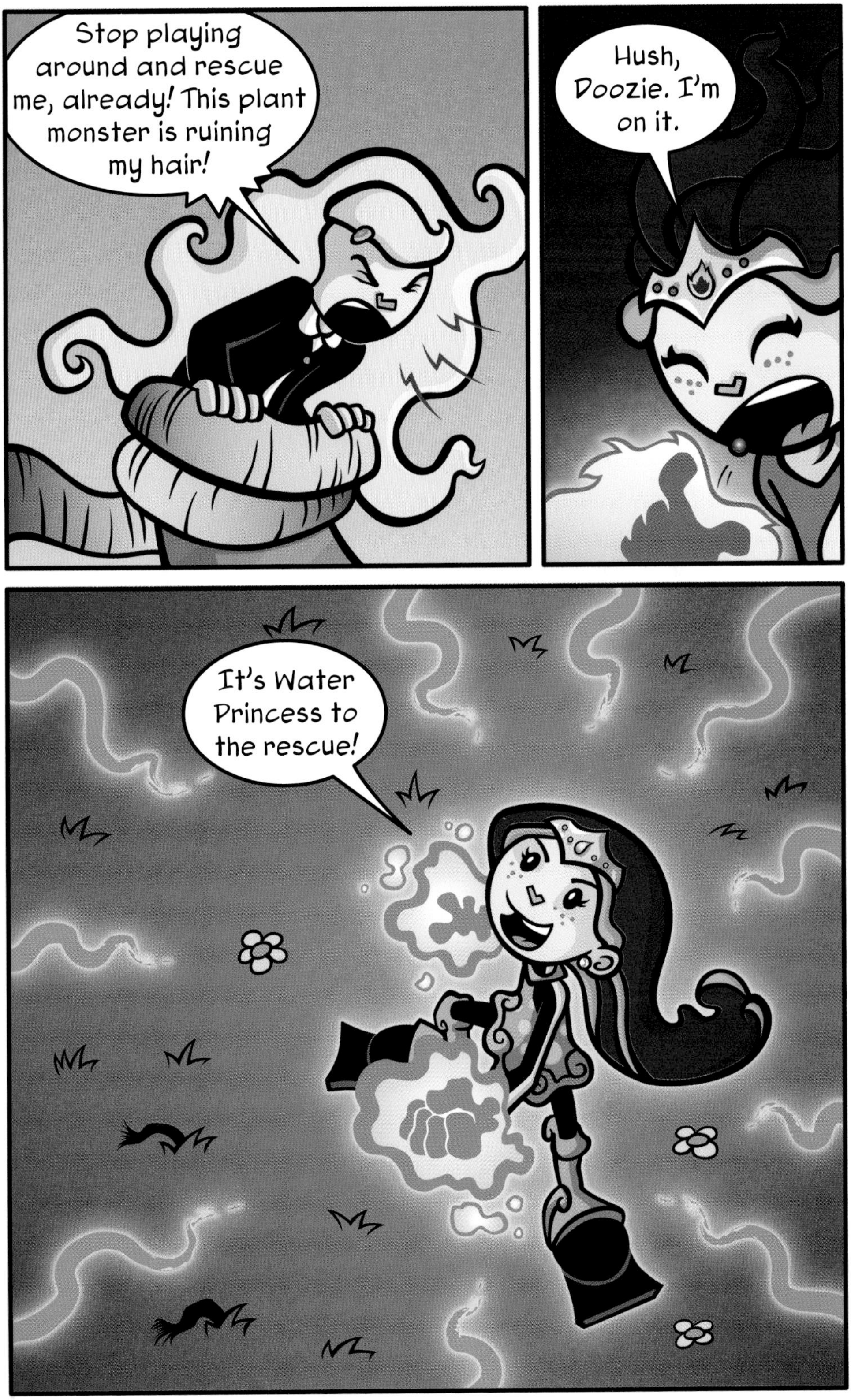
Stop playing around and rescue me, already! This plant monster is ruining my hair!
Hush, Doozie. I'm on it.
It's Water Princess to the rescue!

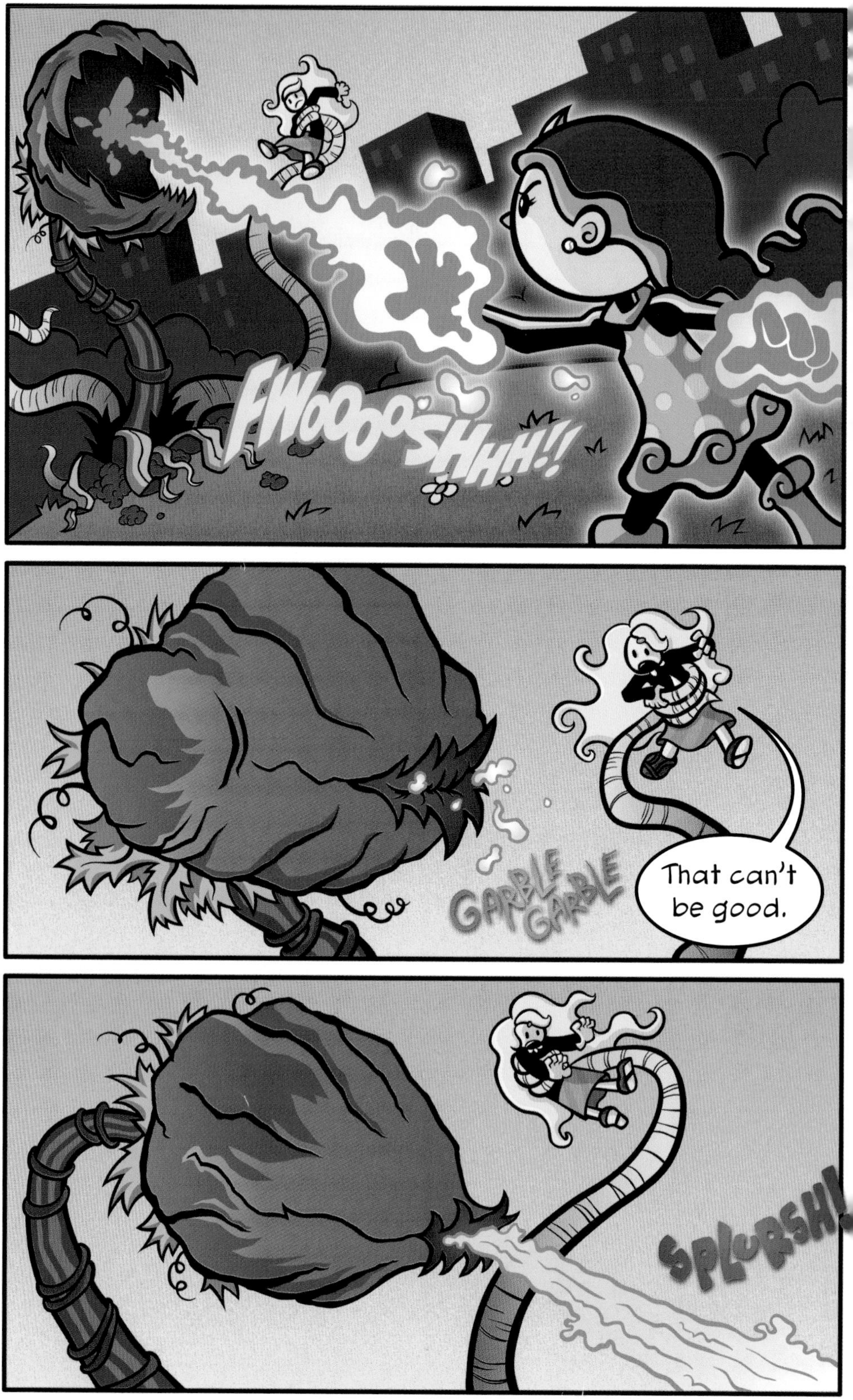
FWOOOOSHHH!!
GARBLE GARBLE
That can't be good.
SPLURSH!

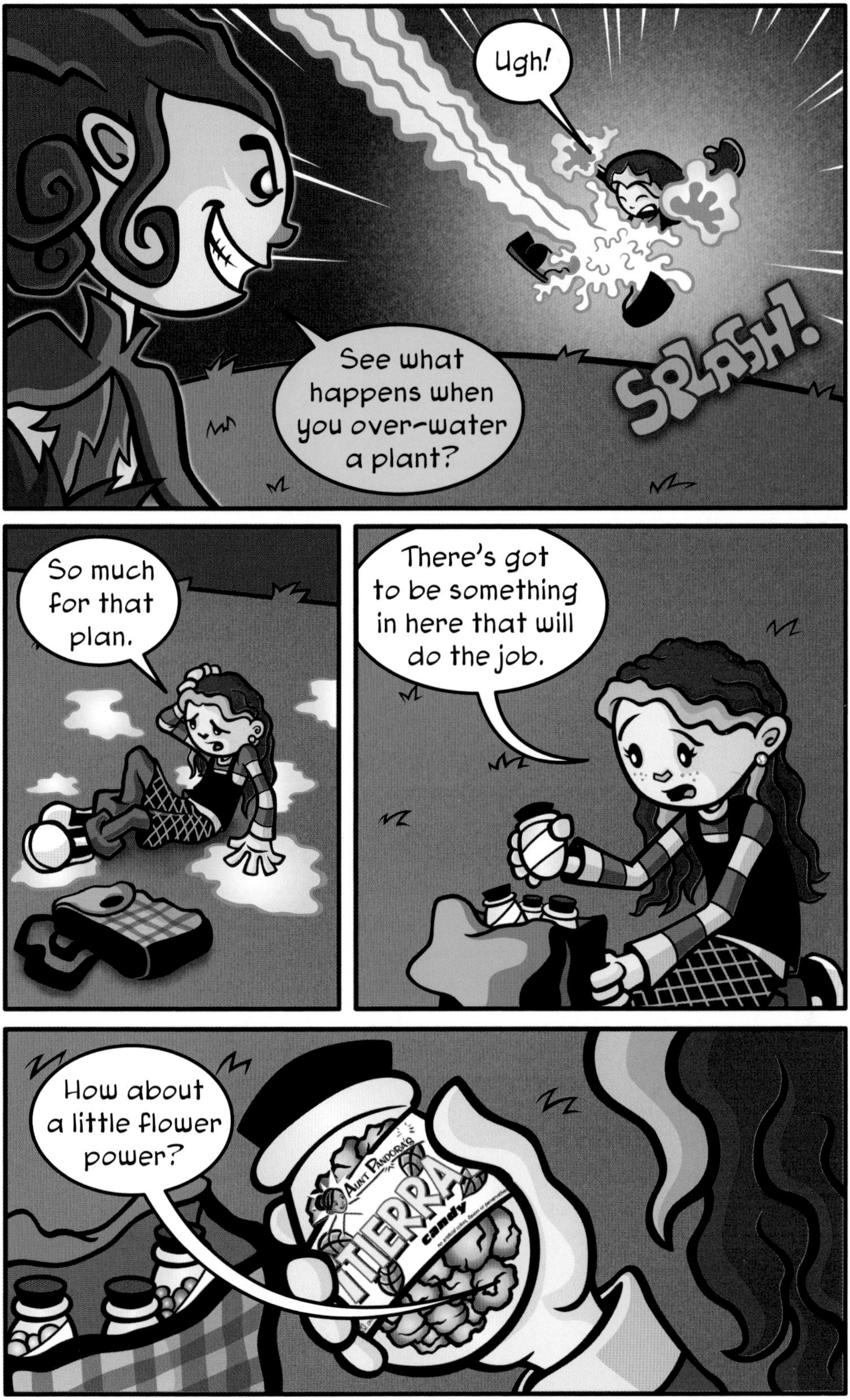
Ugh!
See what happens when you over-water a plant?
SPLASH!
So much for that plan.
There's got to be something in here that will do the job.
How about a little flower power?
AUNT PANDORA'S
TIERRA
candy

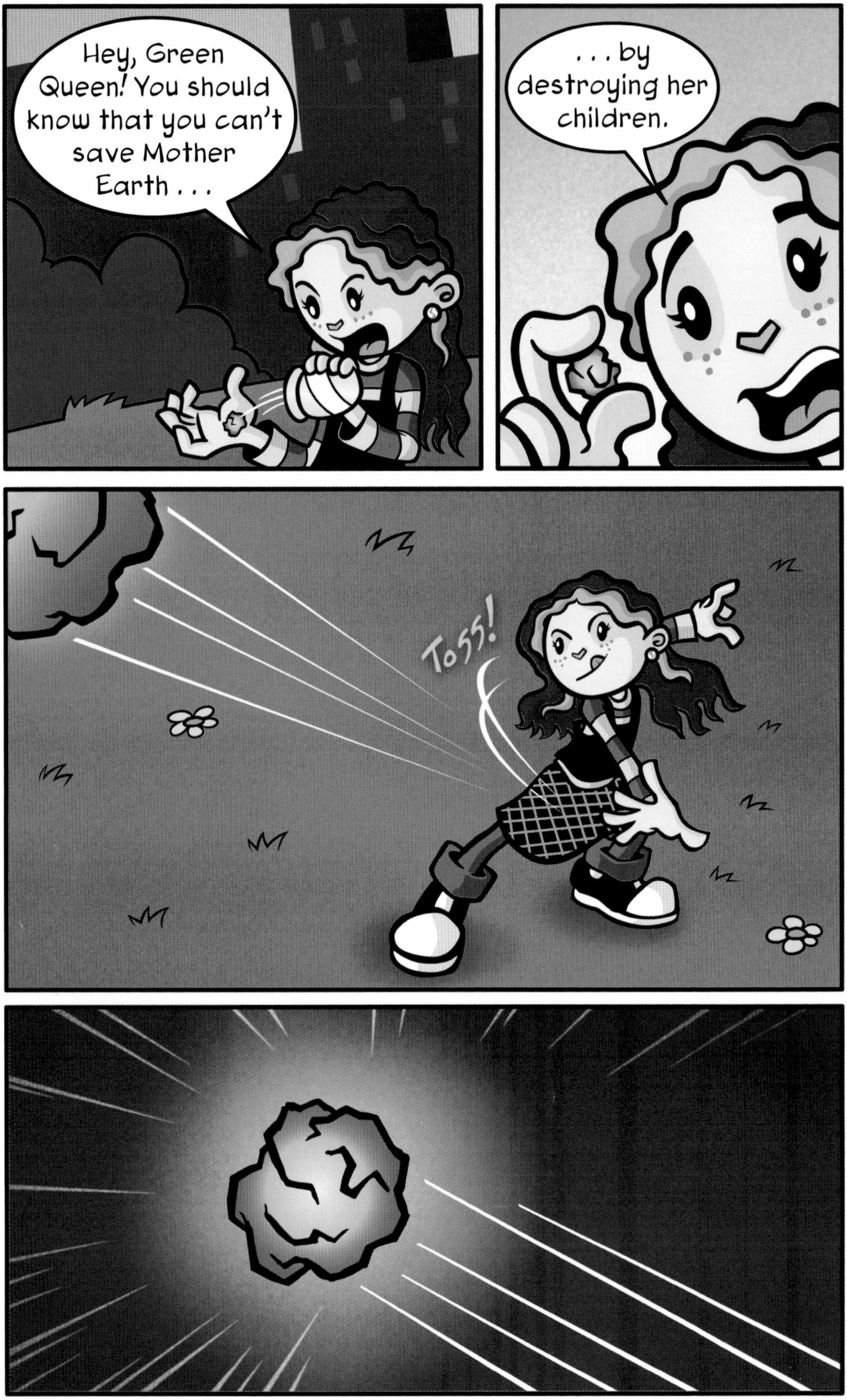
Hey, Green Queen! You should know that you can't save Mother Earth . . .
. . . by destroying her children.
TOSS!

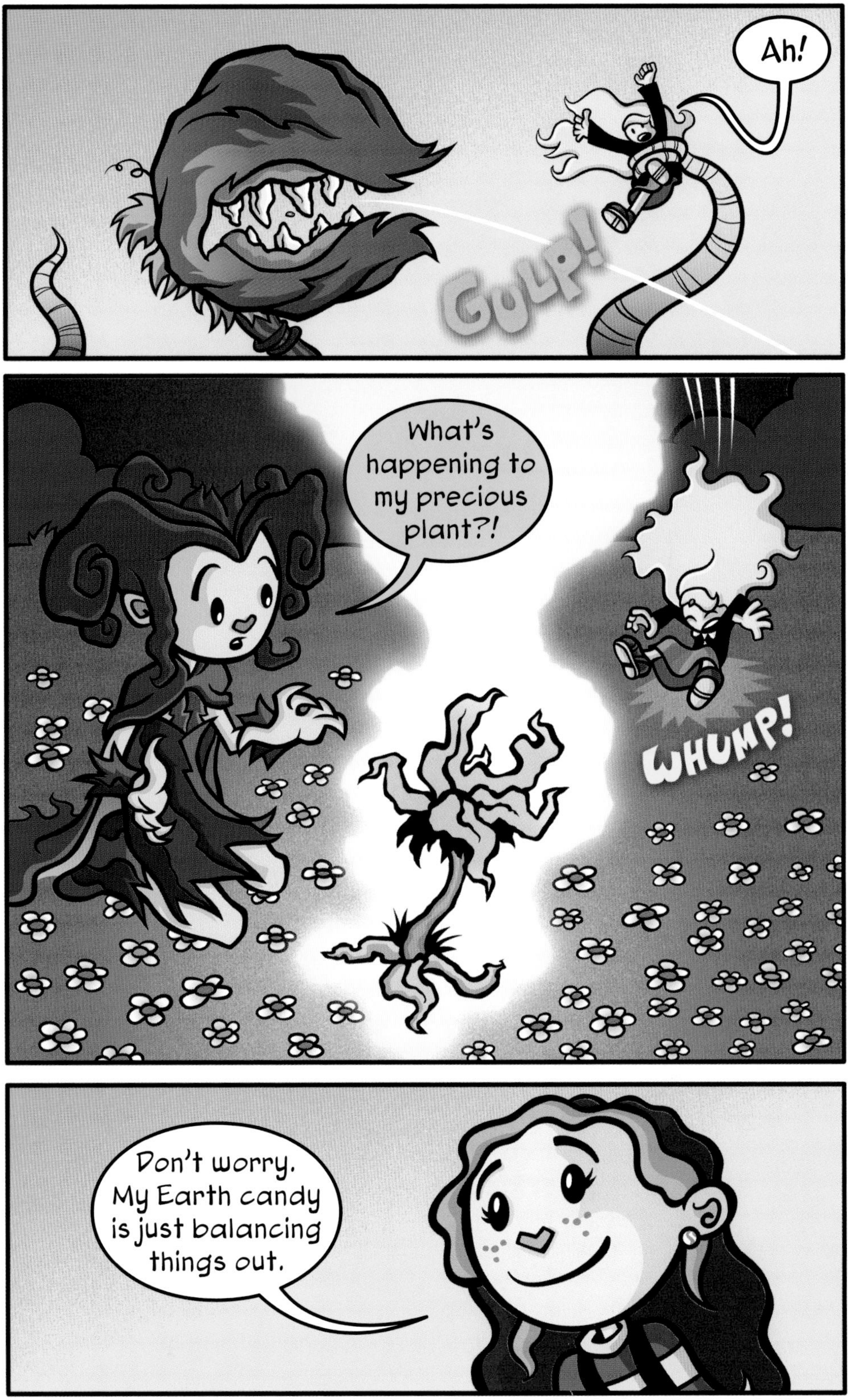
Ah!
GULP!
What's happening to my precious plant?!
WHUMP!
Don't worry. My Earth candy is just balancing things out.

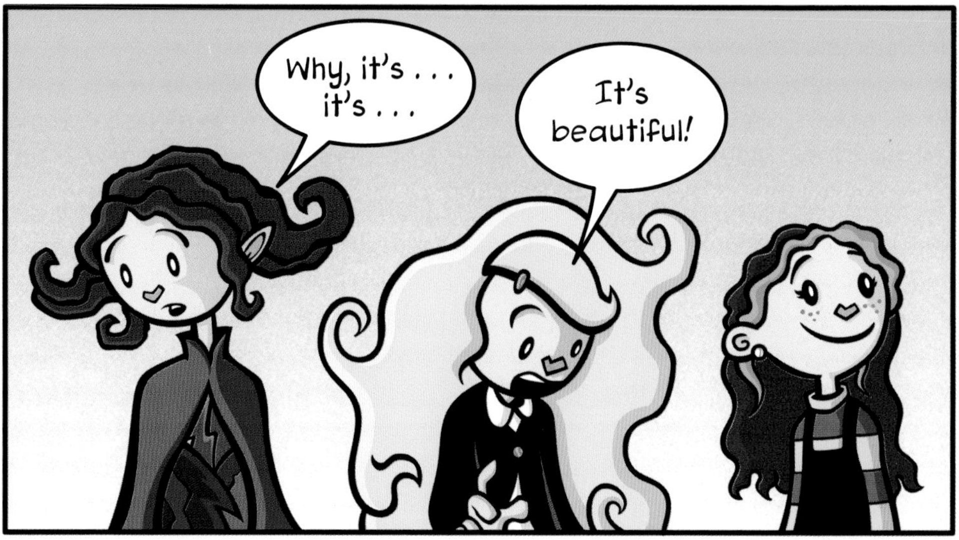
Why, it's . . .
it's . . .
It's beautiful!

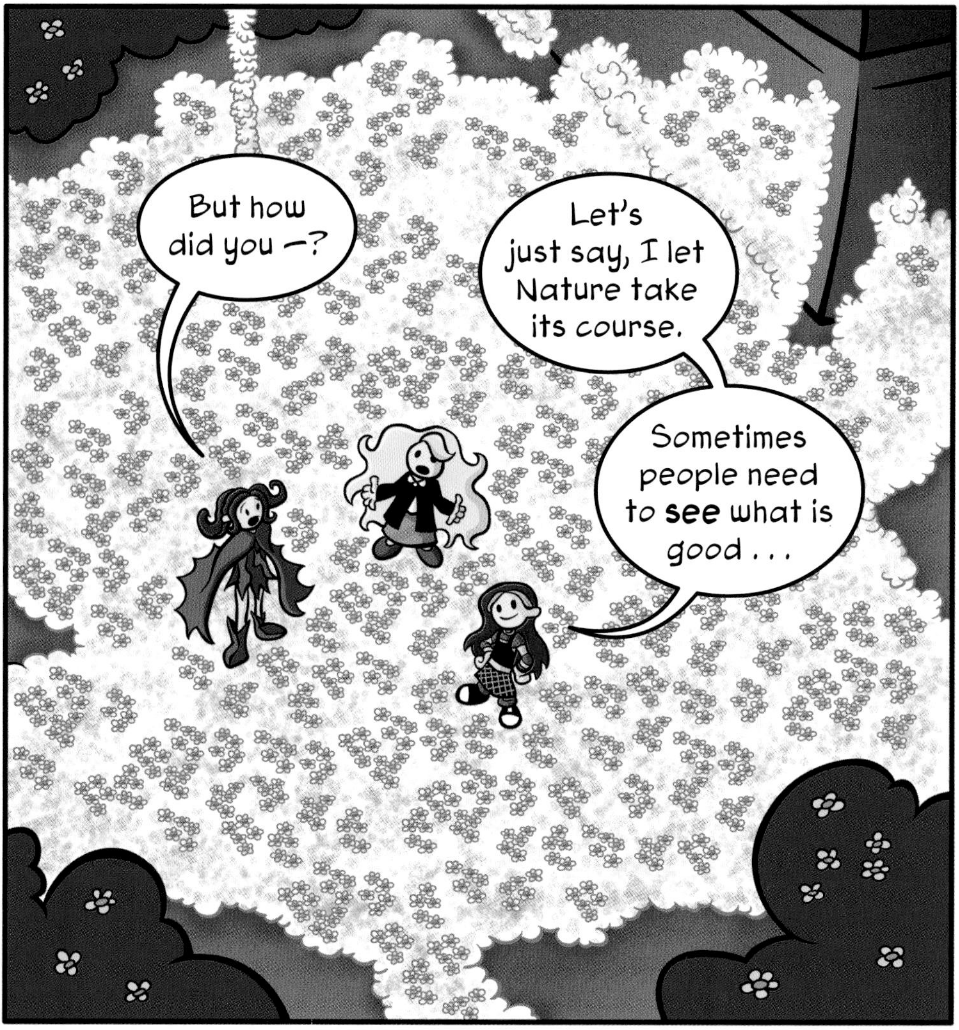
But how did you —?
Let's just say, I let Nature take its course.
Sometimes people need to **see** what is good . . .

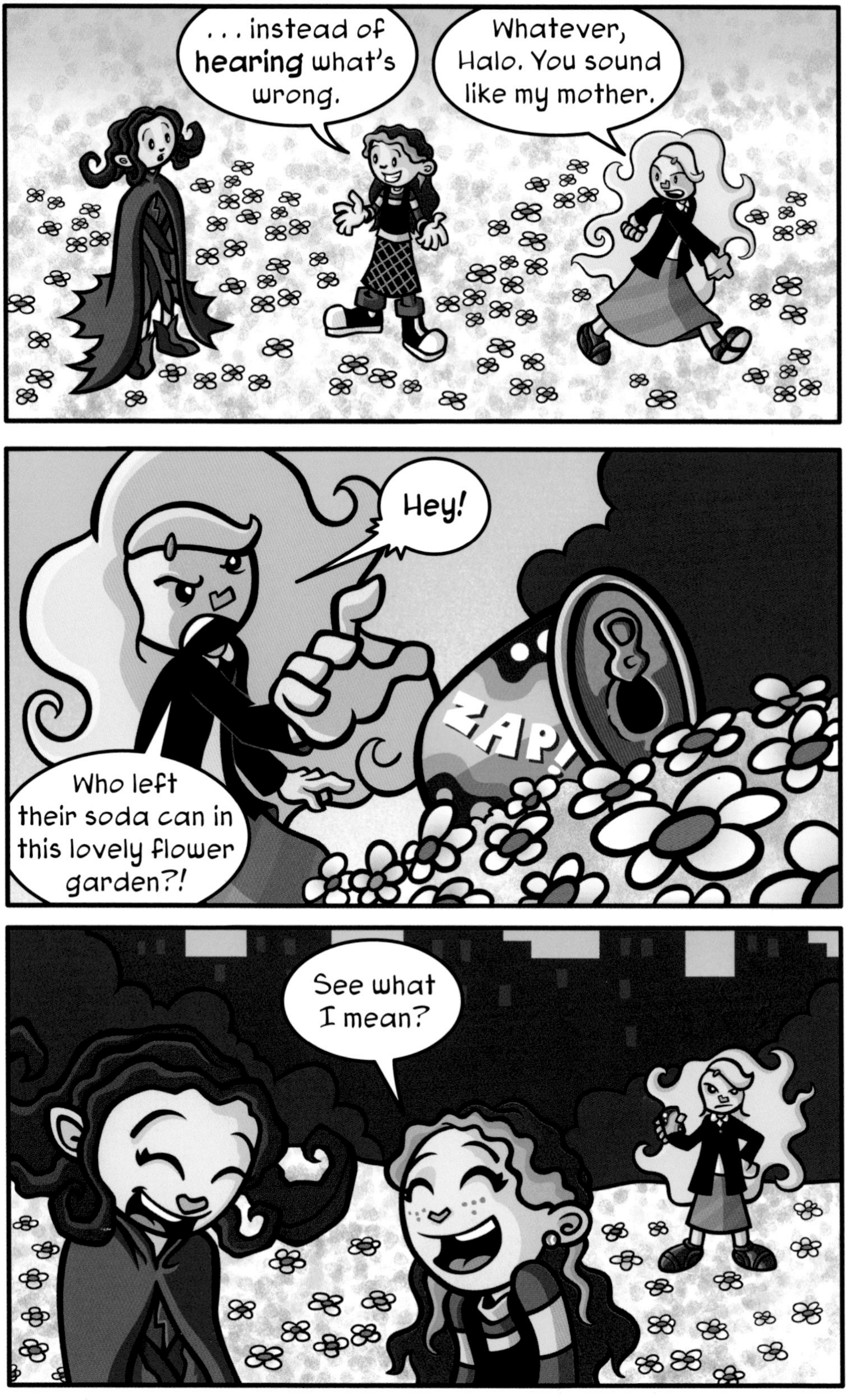
. . . instead of **hearing** what's wrong.
Whatever, Halo. You sound like my mother.
Hey!
Who left their soda can in this lovely flower garden?!
ZAP!
See what I mean?

Green Queen

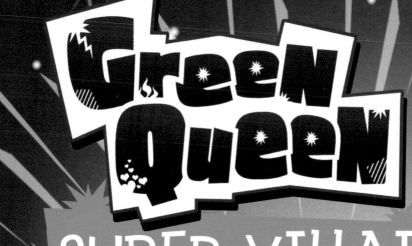

SUPER-VILLAIN

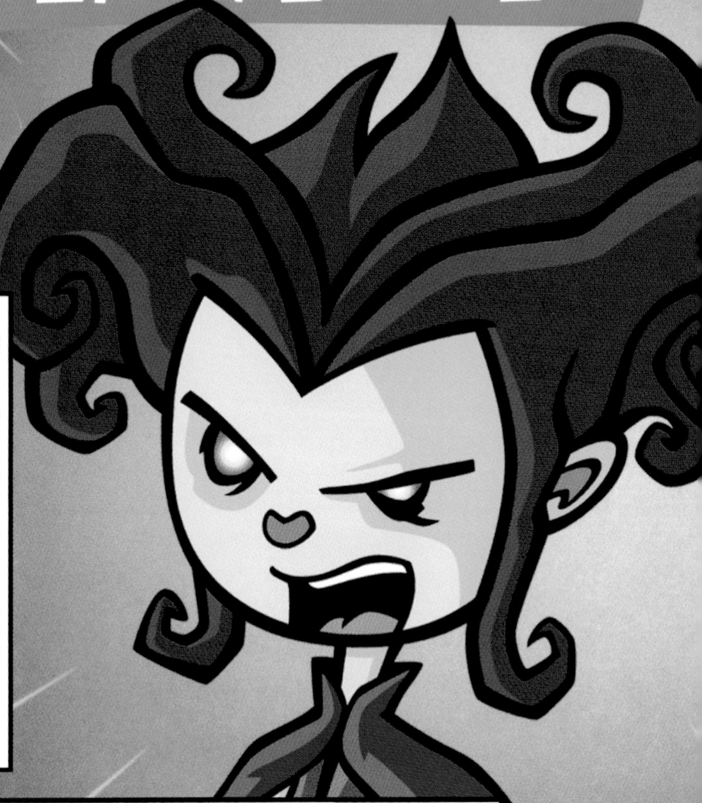

Villain Facts

First Appearance
Princess Candy: Green Queen of Mean

Real Name	Flora Fawn
Occupation	Student, Activist
Height	4 feet 11 inches
Weight	77 pounds
Eyes	Cucumber Green
Hair	Dirt Brown

Special Powers
Can conjure fighting flowers, clinging vines, and snippy Snapdragons. Flora has total control over all things Green.

Most gardeners weed their gardens, but Flora Fawn has a completely different kind of weeding to do. This tree hugger is trying to clean up Mother Earth, but not everyone wants to listen to her helpful tips for saving the planet. Anyone who doesn't heed this high-spirited hippie's warnings faces Flora's recycling rage, transforming her into the ferocious . . . Green Queen! With several vicious plant pets at her disposal, the Green Queen gives new meaning to the phrase "flower power." Enemies of nature beware – the Green Queen won't hesitate to turn litterers into plant food for her leafy minions.

AUNT PANDORA'S

PRINCESS PUZZLERS

Q: How long does it take a non-recycled aluminum can to decompose, or break down, on its own?

A: More than 500 years.

Q: How many trees could be saved every Sunday if everyone recycled their newspapers?

A: 500,000 trees.

Q: How many plastic water bottles are thrown into the trash every day instead of being recycled?

A: An estimated 40 million bottles.

About The Author

Michael Dahl has written more than 200 books for children and young adults. He is the creator of Princess Candy and author of *Sugar Hero* and *The Marshmallow Mermaid*, two other books in the series.

Scott Nickel works at Paws, inc., Jim Davis's famous Garfield studio. He has written dozens of children's books, including *Jimmy Sniffles vs The Mummy*, *Secret of the Summer School Zombies*, and *Wind Power Whiz Kid*. Scott lives in Indiana with his wife, two sons, six cats, and several sea monkeys.

About The Illustrator

Jeff Crowther has been drawing comics for as long as he can remember. Since graduating from college, Jeff has worked on a variety of illustrations for clients including Disney, *Adventures Magazine*, and *Boy's Life* magazine. He also wrote and illustrated the webcomic *Sketchbook* and has self-published several mini-comics. Jeff lives in Boardman, Ohio, with his wife, Elizabeth, and their children, Jonas and Noelle.

Glossary

brilliance (BRIL-yuhnss)—being smart

compost (KOM-pohst)—dead organic matter used to fertilize soil

environment (en-VYE-ruhn-muhnt)—the natural world of the land, sea, and air

fatal (FAY-tuhl)—causing death, or deadly

flash drive (FLASH DRIVE)—a small, high-tech device used to save and store computer files

organic (or-GAN-ik)—using only natural products and no chemicals or pesticides

pollution (puh-LOO-shuhn)—harmful materials that damage or contaminate the air, water, or soil

reduce (ree-DOOSS)—to make something smaller or less

thoughtlessness (THAWT-liss-ness)—if you are thoughtless, you do not consider the consequences of your actions

tree hugger (TREE HUH-guhr)—sometimes used as an insult against people who support protecting the environment

Discussion Question

1. At the end of this book, why do you think Doozie Hiss changed her mind about recycling?

2. Recycling aluminum cans is a good way to help reduce waste. What are some other things you can do to make the world a better place?

3. Halo has to team up with Flora for a class presentation. Do you prefer to do homework alone, or would you rather do group work? Why?

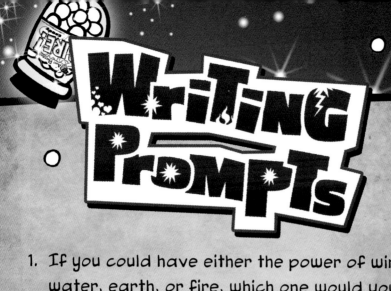

Writing Prompts

1. If you could have either the power of wind, water, earth, or fire, which one would you choose? Why? What would you do with your newfound superpowers?

2. What would have been a better way for Flora to explain how important it is to recycle? Write a letter from Flora to a friend explaining why littering is bad.

3. Imagine that one of Flora's plant creations is out of control, and only Halo can stop it. First, draw a picture of this new plant monster. Then, write a short story about how Halo overcomes her leafy foe!

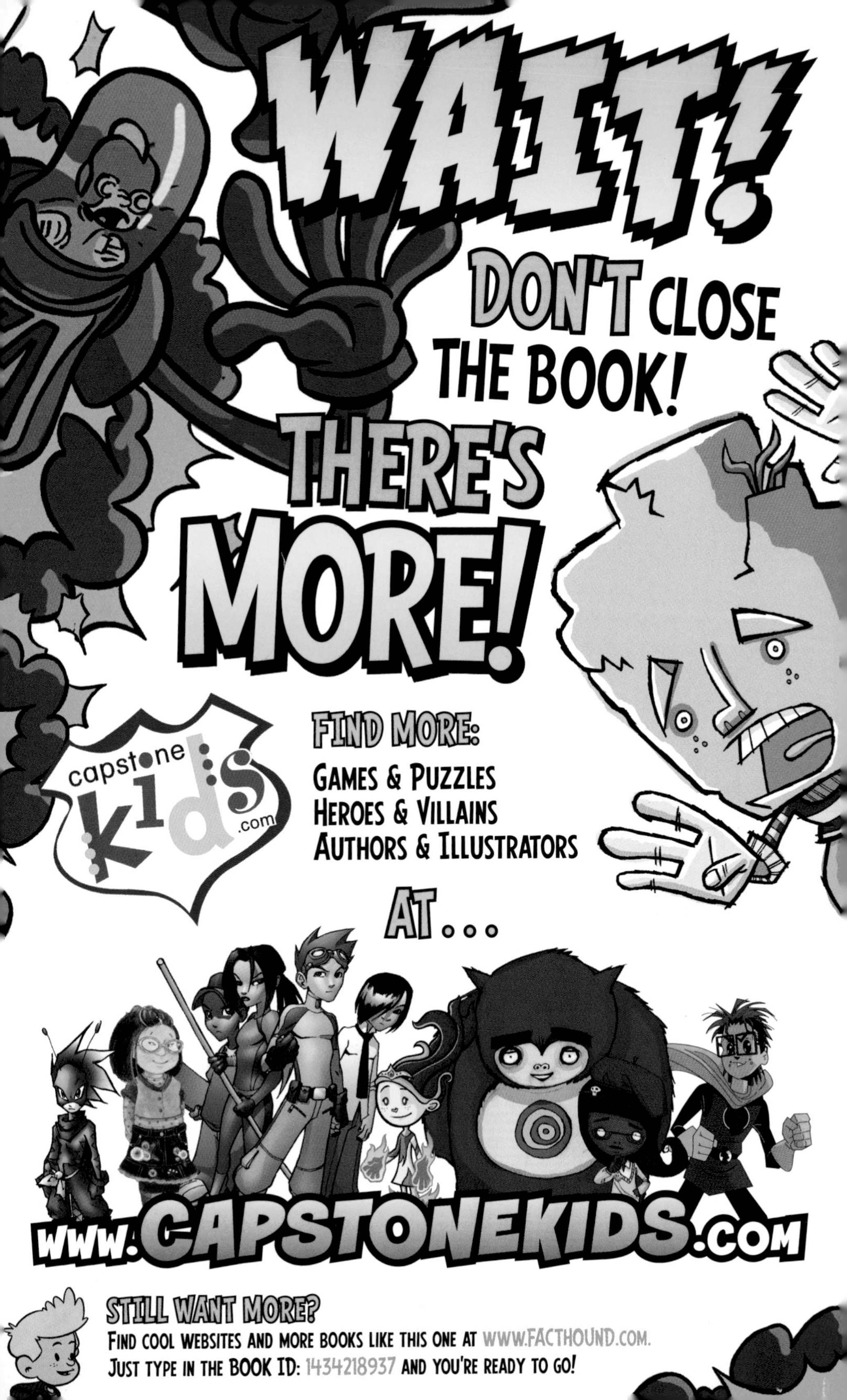
WAIT!
DON'T CLOSE THE BOOK!
THERE'S MORE!
capstone kids .com
FIND MORE:
GAMES & PUZZLES
HEROES & VILLAINS
AUTHORS & ILLUSTRATORS
AT...
WWW.CAPSTONEKIDS.COM
STILL WANT MORE?
FIND COOL WEBSITES AND MORE BOOKS LIKE THIS ONE AT WWW.FACTHOUND.COM.
JUST TYPE IN THE BOOK ID: 1434218937 AND YOU'RE READY TO GO!